REAL MEN HUNT

REAL MEN SHIFT

CELIA KYLE
MARINA MADDIX

DESCRIPTION

She's willing to sacrifice anything to save Wolf Woods from developers--including love. He refuses to let her.

Persia has dedicated her life to saving the planet from greedy construction companies, even if that meant she lost out on a life filled with laughter, love, and passion. Considering she's generally surrounded by losers, potheads, and slackers, it's not such a big loss. Then she meets Warren--a tall, muscular hunk of hottie she wants to climb like the trees she's trying to save.

Werewolf Warren Edgecomb lost out on love once and never imagined he'd find a woman for him. Then he stumbles across Persia and he knows the gorgeous female is *his*. Every curvaceous, delicious, tempting inch of her. The only problem? She's human and can't sense their shifter mate-bond. Plus there's the fact that she likes his wolf better than him.

Warren's only chance of winning over the delectable Persia is to join her protest. Since they both want to bring down the developer attempting to steal his pack's lands, it seems like a match made in heaven. Until he learns a secret that rocks his faith in his instincts--and in Persia.

CHAPTER ONE

"HOW CAN YOU DO THIS TO ME, MOONSHADOW?" THE skinny guy whimpered, still kneeling on the orange shag carpet inside the van. He was probably wearing yet another hole in his canvas pants.

Persia Moonshadow's soon-to-be-very-ex-boyfriend gazed up at her with a plea in his brown eyes, his spindly fingers laced as he begged her not to kick him out. His funky-smelling blond dreadlocks cascaded over his tie-dye-clad shoulders, reaching down his back nearly to his flat ass. Persia wrinkled her nose. How had she ever found the mewling, whiny excuse of a man attractive? One good thing about living in a van with someone—it was a surefire way to fast-track a doomed relationship to the bitter end.

"How many times do I have to tell you, Moonshadow's my *last* name," she replied curtly. She dragged open the door to her ancient Volkswagen Westfalia with a grunt and then slumped onto the back seat.

When they'd first met at a protest a million full moons ago —okay, in reality it was only three—Leaf had decided he liked her last name and was going to call her Moonshadow instead of Persia. Sort of like a nickname, he'd insisted, despite her asking him not to several times. Leaf fancied himself a real hippie, but he'd revealed his true colors over the last three months, and Persia was done.

Leaf blinked slowly in confusion and disbelief, as though he couldn't wrap his mind around how she could possibly want him out. Because he had so much to offer her, of course.

As if.

The warm afternoon breeze had cooled slightly since dusk was falling quickly. Persia took a nice, deep breath to ease her irritation and took a moment to enjoy the way the wind whispered through her soft, red curls. Once her anger was under control, she sighed and gave Leaf a look that broached no argument.

"Time to go."

Or so she thought.

"But, Moonshadow…"

"Persia," she snapped, no longer willing to tolerate his disrespect.

"Persia," he repeated, his face contorting slightly as though her real name was too distasteful for his tongue. "Why are you doing this to me?"

"Not everything is about you, Leaf. That's kind of the problem."

He shot a sideways glance out of the van's open side door at the orange-hued horizon. "But…it's almost nightfall. Where will I go?"

What kind of guy used the word nightfall in conversation? Him, apparently.

"I'm sure one of the others has a sleeping bag you can borrow, and I'll loan you a tarp."

Persia had been in charge of setting up the temporary campsite about a week earlier. Right off the main entrance to a greenspace called Wolf Woods, it was just outside the small Georgia town of Tremble. Most of the protestors she'd recruited had set up tents inside the tree line in an effort to stay off the local cops' radar, but still near the big McNish Development Corporation billboard—the one announcing a new housing development that would decimate the pristine woods. Of course, those with vans had to park in the gravel turnout that acted as a parking lot. That gave Persia a perfect view of the hidden campsite *and* the road, allowing her to be a lookout.

Leaf shimmied a few inches closer, worry she was serious finally settling into his eyes. "But… it gets so cold at night. It's so much warmer here in our van."

"*My* van," she reminded the loser. "You mean *my* van."

"Whatever," he brushed off the concept of ownership. "We all share this big, blue planet, bae. You of all people should know that true enlightenment only comes to those who share."

"Uh huh, and which internet guru fed you that line?"

Persia reached behind the back seat and grabbed a grimy old sweatshirt decorated with an ironic yellow smiley face. She tossed it in Leaf's face. He caught it awkwardly—and ironically, considering his frown—and slung it over his shoulder.

"Come on, Moon—" he quickly caught himself "—Persia. Seriously, I hear there are wolves in these woods." He reached for her hand, but she snatched it away. "Just one more night, baby. One more night and I'll get out in the morning. I swear."

"You are aware the more you beg, the less likely I am to say yes, right?"

Leaf adopted a pained look, as if she'd just shot him in the heart. "What happened to you? What happened to *us*?"

Once upon a time, that soft, sensitive expression had made her weak in the knees. Now it annoyed her.

Crossing her arms, she decided it was time to call his bluff.

"I have just one question for you, Leaf. Do you even like me?"

Persia knew Leaf didn't love her, just as she didn't love him. One benefit of living to the ripe old age of twenty-eight meant she recognized when a relationship was a short-term thing. And Leaf had been short-term from the very beginning. He only dragged it out now because he didn't want to sleep on the ground.

Wimp!

His hesitation was all the answer she needed.

"Actually, you know what? You can find someone else to borrow a tarp from. I think I'll keep mine."

Leaf's mouth fell open, stunned.

"Out," she spat and pointed at the open door.

Leaf's demeanor turned cold as he crawled out of the van. He stood outside the door, hands on his skinny hips, and glared at her. "You know what? You're a real bitch."

"And don't you forget it." She smiled and chucked his backpack at him.

Leaf lingered for a moment and then wandered toward the hidden campsite in search of shelter for the night. Who needed a television when watching Leaf beg for handouts was so immensely entertaining? Someone finally handed over a tarp, then another someone apparently had a sleeping bag to spare. They'd be sorry when he returned it smelling of his white-boy dreads.

What a user, just like everyone else in this ugly, fucking world of theirs. Good riddance!

Still, Leaf was well-liked among the protestors, and Persia was in no mood to sit around waiting for the inevitable tidal wave of gossip. Shrugging into her favorite Oompa Loompa sweatshirt, she pulled her walking stick from its overhead holder and climbed out of the van. She locked the doors before heading into the woods she was so committed to protecting.

Handmade signs shouting *KEEP WOLF WOODS WILD* and *DOWN WITH DICK*—referencing Dick McNish, the owner of the McNish Development Corporation—sat propped against tree trunks and tents. Not far away, bulldozers sat idly, menacing reminders their protest wasn't going as well as they'd hoped. Not that a little pushback from Dick McNish would stop her. She'd seen worse. *Much* worse.

Once the lush forest surrounded her, Persia could finally breathe again. The deeper she pushed into the woods, the lighter her heart felt, until she suddenly realized she was singing her favorite song, *Endless Love*. The Luther Vandross and Mariah Carey version, not the original, though that was good, too.

None of her new-agey boyfriends had ever understood her fondness for sappy love songs, but Persia had a penchant for surprising people. It kept them on their toes and made them wonder what she'd do next. The last thing she wanted was for anyone to pin down exactly who she was and what made her tick. She preferred to remain an enigma. Wrapped in mystery.

Nature had a way of curing whatever heartache or stress ailed Persia. Nothing compared to being completely alone in the woods, the birds in the trees harmonizing with her terrible singing. Her troubles seemed to melt away with every step she took, until she was totally blissed out. So blissed out, in fact, her brain didn't quite register what she was seeing when she stumbled across a huge, beautiful clearing in the woods.

"My…endless…" She stopped singing mid-chorus, eyes popping wide.

An absolutely enormous beast crouched in the center of the clearing, not twenty feet away from where she lurched to a stop. A wolf. With sandy-colored fur. And gleaming blue eyes.

Oh.

My.

God.

Persia's blood ran cold as the wolf stared at her. Then her heart thundered in her chest while options flitted through her brain at the speed of terror. No way could she outrun an animal that big—hell, with her short legs and extra poundage, she wouldn't have been able to outrun a freaking mini-dachshund. But it wasn't as if there was a panic room handy. She didn't have much choice. She'd have to make a run for it. Better than standing around waiting to become wolf chow.

Panic seized her, but before she could spin and bolt back into the woods, the wolf's next action froze her where she stood. He laid down and rested his stupidly huge head on his stupidly huge paws. *Oh hey, I'm just a wolf taking a nap. Nothing to see here.*

Sure.

Persia remembered Little Red Riding Hood. She knew the score.

But the way he looked at her, all big-eyed and gentle, gave her pause. His blue gaze never wavered, almost as if he was curious rather than ravenous. It wasn't like she had a lot of experience with wild animals, but she knew enough about wolves to acknowledge that his behavior wasn't exactly typical.

Then it got even weirder. The beast let out a plaintive little whine and then rolled over on his back to expose his soft underbelly. He stared at her from his upside-down position and panted, his tongue lolling out as he looked at her almost… expectantly?

No way. That couldn't be. Time to stop ogling and start running. But just as she prepared to turn, the fear that consumed her just vanished in a single heartbeat. The panic had been replaced with certain understanding that the wolf had no intention of harming her.

Before she even knew she was doing it, Persian leaned forward a bit. "Do you want me to rub your belly?"

What.

The.

Fuck.

That was a dumb question. Wild wolves didn't go around begging strange humans to rub their tummies. This was some kind of apex predator trap. It had to be. But her gut told her it wasn't, despite what her brain insisted. Almost as if confirming her instincts, the wolf seemed to smile, his big, bushy tail wagging happily.

Fully aware she acted like a crazy person, but unable to resist, Persia slowly approached the wolf. She held her walking stick out in front of her as if the brittle piece of wood might protect her. When she got close enough, she set it down and knelt beside the gigantic wolf. He still hadn't moved from his upside-down position, so she raised one trembling hand and tentatively petted the wolf's stomach. His silken fur was so soft and warm beneath her palm and he appeared to enjoy the attention, as bizarre as that seemed.

"Wow," she breathed and shook her head in disbelief. "You really like this. Don't you?"

The wolf simply gazed at her with what could only be described as affection. If a guy had ever looked at her that way, she would have married him in an instant. Thick fur resisted her fingers, but the deeper she dug and scratched, the happier he seemed.

"This is weird as hell. But hey, who am I to turn up my nose at a new friend? I'm Persia Moonshadow. I wish you could tell me your name."

The wolf groaned and shifted slightly so her fingers could access an itch, and then his hind leg started thumping the air.

"Oh, that's the spot, huh?" she chuckled.

Most dogs had "that" spot, the one that made their back leg go crazy. Persia never would have believed she'd find such a spot on a strange wolf. Yet, he wasn't strange at all. Something about the creature seemed almost familiar. Like they were old pals. And just as she would with a friend, she started venting to him. It wasn't as if he had problems of his own to unload on her. So why not?

"Dude, you wouldn't believe the day I've had. Protesting all day, to no effect, of course. Then I found out my boyfriend stole my debit card to buy weed—*again*—and I finally kicked his ass to the curb. Oh, don't feel bad for me. He was just another user. Leaf—yeah, you heard me right… *Leaf*—was never primo dating material anyway. More someone to pass the time with, you know? Three months wasted on another loser. Again."

The wolf still gazed at her intently, like he actually listened. And understood.

"The worst part is, he wasn't even that bad, compared to some of the assholes I've dated. God, I'm so sick of passive, whiny, wimpy guys who leech off me for their food and shelter while they sit around playing their harmonicas or bongo drums or, god forbid, didgeridoos. Oh, and smoking a ton of grass, too. Which, whatever, but we're trying to save a forest here. It's serious business. This isn't Burning Man. Know what I mean? But they never see it the way I do. They all talk a big game about how much they love the environment, blah blah blah, but eventually their true colors show. That's when I know it's time to kick 'em out."

The wolf panted and blinked, waiting for her to continue. Persia rolled her eyes.

"Most of these guys don't give a shit about anything but themselves. Protesting is just an excuse not to have a job, if you ask me. And to not shower," she added, wrinkling her nose.

"The worst part is how many girls lap that shit up like milk. They fall for all that green, hippie crap. But not me. Nope. I only hooked up with Leaf because, let's be real, protesting is tough work. It can be isolating and lonely. A girl's got needs, you know? Not that any of those guys were ever good in the sack anyway."

The one-way conversation lit a bulb over Persia's head. "You know, screw it. Men are just distractions. I'm done with them. For good."

The wolf whined and rolled back onto his tummy, resting his head in her lap and looking up at her with pleading eyes.

"I know. I know." She stroked his giant head. "But I have more important matters to focus on. Like saving Wolf Woods."

The wolf wriggled closer and licked her face, stunning Persia for a moment before she started giggling.

"You are a sweetheart. Aren't you?" She buried her hands deep into the fur on either side of his head and grinned. Then she glanced up at the darkening sky overhead. "Crap. It's getting late. I need to get back to the campsite so I can get ready for work."

Releasing her new woodland buddy, she stood and brushed wolf hair off her clothing. The wolf cocked his head in a silent, very judgy question.

"What? It's not like protesting is a high-paying gig, my friend. A girl's gotta eat, ya know." As she turned to head back to her van, she glanced back at the wolf, who'd sat up to watch her departure intently. "It was, um, nice to make your acquaintance, Mr. Wolf. I hope you have a good night."

AN HOUR LATER, SURROUNDED BY SMOKE AND ANNOYINGLY blaring country music, Persia slid a tray of beers off the counter of The Wolf's Lair Bar and Grille. Her new temporary boss, Hux Davenport, gave her a congenial nod. Thank goodness it was a slow night, so she didn't have to weave and dodge a bunch of good ol' boys. She made her way to a table in the corner where two old-timers sat deep in conversation.

"Don't you get it, Chuck?" the old guy with the red hunting cap spoke. "We need to protect what's ours, not let some damn fool like Dick McNish come in and cut it all down. Wolf Woods has been wild since... forever. Besides, you know as well as I do how much money these idiot werewolf seekers spend in town, just for a chance to walk in those damn woods."

Chuck shook his head, as if his companion was the biggest idiot in Tremble. "That ain't nothing compared to jobs, Hank."

Oh lord, not *that* old chestnut! Persia, who'd never been very good at holding her tongue, couldn't help herself.

"Actually," she interrupted, startling both of the men who seemed to not have noticed her presence, "any jobs McNish brings in will be temporary, at best. And trust me, those very temporary jobs won't go to locals. He's known for bringing in his own crews, who cost way less in the long run. Even if he does hire *some* locals, the work will only last until the houses in his cookie-cutter development are built. And then you've lost the steady tourist dollars forever."

"See?" the man named Hank crowed at his pal. "Even *she* knows how it works.

Chuck's face flamed red with fury at being upstaged by some stupid waitress. "Yeah, like some libtard bitch has any idea what she's talking about!"

"You callin' me a bitch?" Hank thundered, jumping to his feet as his chair spun across the floor from the sudden move.

"No, I'm calling *her* a bitch," Chuck snarled, slowly standing and clenching his ham-sized fists. "I'm calling *you* a fuckin' dumbass!"

Oops! If Persia had just kept her big mouth shut, she wouldn't have to break up a fight between a couple of drunk codgers.

"Guys, can we please take it down a notch?" Persia pleaded, stepping between them and flashing a wobbly smile. Men usually went crazy for her dimples.

But the men were already moving, and before she even knew what happened, a plaid-covered elbow connected sharply with her forehead. That sent her flying back into the wall with a painful thud before she bounced off and her head bashed against the side of a table. Then the lights went out and the world went dark.

CHAPTER TWO

WARREN EDGECOMB PULLED INTO THE PARKING LOT OF The Lair, turned down the lazy melody of the country song he sang along to and rolled his windows up before anyone heard his terrible voice. He brought the truck to a stop in a parking spot with lines so faded only locals knew where they were and took a deep breath.

*Warren, you're getting ahead of yourself again.*It was just light enough to see bats flitting around between the swaying trees, having their nightly dinner. Watching bats and fireflies always settled Warren down when he felt out of sorts. Tonight, though, they weren't cutting it.

How could they? It wasn't every day a guy went out for a walk in the woods and ran into his fated mate. Not even a shred of doubt lingered in Warren's heart that he had, indeed, finally found his mate. If he'd been in his human form when they'd stumbled across each other in Wolf

Woods earlier, he might have questioned their connection, but his wolf knew better. The beast recognized her in an instant, and his entire world had turned upside down.

Warren had always had a good head on his shoulders. Dependable, even-tempered, smart. Just like any good ol' country boy should be. He felt confident as the beta for the Soren pack, their lands located just on the other side of Wolf Woods. He'd never doubted his abilities to serve the pack and their alpha, Zeke Soren.

But a love life? Yeah, no.

The strangest part of it all was that he hadn't just been wandering around the off-limits Wolf Woods for fun when he'd caught Persia's scent on the wind and followed it to the clearing. Dick McNish had greased every palm he could to secure the rights to rip out the woods for the sake of some generic, cookie-cutter condos.

The pack had thought they'd won when a large newspaper had published a scathing exposé accusing the real estate developer of pulling shady crap all over Georgia. Then McNish had brought in an army of bulldozers—okay, three—to intimidate them.

It was a mind-fuck, and they all knew it. Unfortunately, it had also been quite effective. Apparently so had the article. After moving the dozers to the parking lot of the woods, not another peep had been heard. It seemed McNish had gone into his own personal form of hiding.

He'd been a thorn in the pack's side for far too long. Not a thorn, more like a loaded gun trained directly at the pack. Literally. Considering McNish had ordered one of his goons to shoot a Soren pup, along with any other wolves they ran across, the pack knew better than to breathe easy as long as he was out there, ready to stir up trouble. So Zeke had sent Warren out to make sure McNish hadn't revved up his bulldozers.

As he'd been heading back to Soren pack lands after seeing the slumbering dozers, he'd scented his mate and stopped dead in his tracks. It didn't seem possible, not after his heart had been so shattered when his childhood crush had found her own mate, but once he'd caught sight of her, any doubt had vanished. She was his.

And she'd taken his breath away. Flowing red curls topped the loveliest, creamiest skin he'd ever seen. His sharp wolf eyes had been able to see the smattering of freckles across the bridge of her nose, even at a distance, and her plump pink lips begged to be kissed. When she'd drawn closer, he'd been mesmerized by her eyes—one blue, one brown—and the fact she'd seemed to trust him, a strange wolf in the woods.

As a wolf, he stood as tall as her waist, but in human form, he would tower over her short frame by a good foot, not that such a height disparity bothered him in the slightest.

But her abundant curves had really started his wolf panting. Breasts out to there, tucking into a trim waist and flaring back out generously where her hips started.

But there was more to his mate than mere appearances. He'd caught the faint scent of patchouli on her, as if she'd been near someone wearing it, coupled with a gauzy, flowing skirt that hugged her hips beautifully and a thin tank top which showed off what her mama had given her —without the benefit of a bra, praise be—told him she had to be one of the protestors trying to save Wolf Woods. The females he'd grown up with wore camo and rode ATVs while Persia probably had a dreamcatcher hanging over her bed. Or tent, more than likely.

Not that her status as an environmentalist bothered Warren either. Wolves in general leaned in that direction, purely to maintain their ancestral pack lands. It didn't really matter why they were both fighting against McNish, just that they were on the same side.

What worried him more was that his mate was a human. Of course, some of his favorite pack mates used to be human, but *she* might have a problem with him being a werewolf. Humans didn't always react well when they learned werewolves were real.

Even worse, he'd presented himself to her in his wolf form, and now she saw him as an overgrown pet rather than her life mate. He could still feel her fingers buried in his fur, staring into his eyes with her bi-colored ones, and a shiver of need rolled through him. He'd just have to track her down, woo her in his human form and pretend to be something he wasn't, which presented its own sort of difficulty.

Warren's luck had run out in the love department, and he certainly didn't have many skills at flirting. He'd grown a lot since letting go of his immature crush on Zeke's sister, Chloe. One of the things he'd learned was that he'd need to be open and honest with his future mate, should he ever be lucky enough to find one. Now that he had, he realized how hard that would be as a wolf trying to court a human.

He'd tried following her at a safe distance, but too many campers had been milling around. Sadly, most humans reacted to wolves exactly as Persia had initially—with fear. Besides, even though they hadn't seen any of McNish's wolf hunters out for a few days, that didn't mean they weren't prowling around, just itching to spill some wolf blood.

After high-tailing it to the pack house, he'd driven his truck back to the entrance of Wolf Woods in search of his ginger mate. Even before he'd opened his door, he knew Persia wasn't there. Her scent, an intoxicating mix of cotton candy and berries, had lingered in the air though, so he knew she'd only recently left. Time to ask around.

Venturing into the woods where most of the protestors were camping, Warren had looked around for anyone who looked friendly. A scrawny slip of a man with nasty blond dreadlocks had been lying on his back under a flimsy blue tarp tied to the side of a tree, taking a pull off a vape pen. Something about the kid had set Warren's teeth on edge, which the fellow must have sensed because as soon as their eyes had met, the boy's brown ones grew wide and he scooted back on his ratty sleeping bag until he was hidden from Warren's view.

"Greetings," a willowy brunette had spoken as she heated a pot of something resembling food over a small propane stove. "Are you joining us for dinner?"

Her stoned boyfriend had smiled lazily as he plucked out a gentle tune on his guitar. Warren had returned their smiles as he shook his head.

"Thanks, but I'm looking for a pretty redhead. I think her name's Persia?"

He hadn't been able to bring himself to speak her obviously fake last name, Moonshadow. Thankfully he hadn't needed to.

"Sorry, she took off about an hour ago."

"Right, she mentioned something about going to work, but I can't for the life of me remember where," Warren inserted as smoothly as he could. A cop would have seen right through him, but the trusting hippies had taken him at face value.

"The Lair, man," the woman's boyfriend had crooned, almost in tune with his music.

That was all Warren had needed to know.

"Are you sure you don't want some lentils?" the woman had called after him in a wistful tone as he hurried back to his truck, ignoring her.

As he sat in his truck, watching The Lair's red and yellow neon flickering, he wondered if marching into his newfound and totally unsuspecting mate's place of work was such a bright idea. Everything in him screamed to run in and find her, just to make sure she was safe, but the human half of him knew he'd have to go slowly. Not only was she a human who had no idea werewolves existed, but she'd told him not an hour earlier that she was swearing off men for good. If he ran in calling her his mate and claiming to be a werewolf, she'd call the dudes in the white coats.

Warren dragged his palm over his face and sighed. Of course, it would be his luck that he'd have to go through the human channels to get things done. But for his mate, he'd do anything.

"Persia." He tested how the name sounded on his tongue.

Pretty, perky, bold.

Just like her.

With a breath for luck, he hopped out of his truck and headed around the building, only to find the most quintessential Tremble scene ever. Levi Walker, the pack's former enforcer and a town cop, stood in front of the building, his arms crossed across his broad chest as he listened to an inebriated older fellow blather on. The man's wispy white beard bobbed as he spoke, his soiled work jeans, muddy boots, and a sweat-stained red-and-black flannel shirt under black suspenders a typical good ol' boy uniform. The man swayed slightly as his arms flailed.

As Warren walked past the pair, the man spat a wad of black goo into the dirt and used his tongue to push a nasty lump of chew back into place in his lower lip before continuing his ramble at Levi. Warren had trouble catching everything he slurred, thanks to his thick Georgia accent coupled with slurring.

"Occifer, I tells ya, Chuck done hit her good wit his elbow. I seen it. You go on an' look. I seen it! Git her looked at so you can enter it in ev-ee-dence, tell you what."

"Sir," Levi sounded weary, "if you could please…"

Whatever came after that, Warren didn't hear it. The insistent thunder of his quickened heartbeat drowned out everything else. The redneck's words were nonsense, yet Warren's belly cramped at each one. Somehow, Persia was involved. If there was one thing Warren had learned in the hour or so since encountering his mate, it was that he needed to listen to his gut.

Throwing open the door to The Lair, he stopped in the doorway and nearly shifted with rage. Hux Davenport, the owner of the bar and a Soren pack member, squatted over a motionless Persia, fanning a dirty dishtowel in her face. Whatever had happened to her, Hux's ministrations didn't seem to be working because she was completely knocked out. A trickle of blood dribbled down her forehead and into her hair.

Hux glanced behind him, his eyes growing wide at Warren's presence. Not because he was there, but because he was snarling in Hux's general direction. The man scooted away, leaving the human female for Warren to deal with.

Smart man.

Rushing to her, Warren held her oval face in his hands and breathed deeply. Yes, his mate. No question. And she was injured. *Damn it!*

Scooping her into his arms, Warren marveled at her fragility and vowed to make it his life's mission to keep her safe, forevermore. As he turned to head out the door, Levi stepped back inside and gave him a bewildered look. The old redneck peered over his shoulder at the scene.

"What the hell, Warren," Levi hissed under his breath. "I already called an ambulance. You can't just—"

Warren didn't need to say a word. He just gave Levi a look as hard as steel, and the man backed off. He even held the door open for Warren as he carried her to his truck. She needed treatment from one of the few people in the world he trusted.

His sister.

CHAPTER THREE

Persia's eyes fluttered open and then narrowed at the bright lights beaming over her head. Squinting them shut again, she winced at the pounding throb in her brain. Headaches were one thing, but the pain stabbing into her head like a knife with every heartbeat far surpassed anything she'd ever experienced.

What the hell happened?

Thinking back to the last event she could clearly recall, she retraced her steps. Kicking Leaf out of her van. A walk in the woods. A wolf.

Wait.

A wolf? Did it attack her?

Her heart sped up, making the ache in her brain twice as painful. It only slowed down when the wolf's sharp blue eyes penetrated the murderous throbbing in her head. No, he'd rolled over and snuggled her like she'd raised him from a puppy. Her new woodland friend.

Finally, back on track, she remembered going to work at The Lair. Something about a couple of old rednecks tickled the back of her brain, but the poor organ couldn't manage to bring up that particular memory, and the more she tried, the more she hurt.

"Mmmf," she groaned as she peeled her eyes open against the light again.

It looked more like an adjustable lamp found in hospitals. The harsh smell of antiseptic added to the impression. Whatever had happened to her, someone must have taken her to a doctor's office or urgent care. Persia tried turning her head to get a look around the space, sending a jolt of pain through her body. Bad idea. Maybe sitting up would be easier.

Grunting with effort, she fumbled for the side of the bed, only to find hand rails. It was a gurney. Perfect for keeping her steady as she slowly pushed herself into a sitting position. The room tilted this way and that, so she closed her eyes until she didn't feel as if she was standing on the bow of a tiny boat in stormy seas.

"Oh good, you're awake," a soft, feminine voice came from nearby.

Cracking one eye open, Persia looked at the tall, fairly fuzzy woman who approached. A few blinks cleared her vision enough to see the woman was also breathtakingly beautiful—the kind of woman elderly billionaires left entire estates to. But something about her presence calmed Persia. If this woman was her doctor, she was in good hands.

"Who…what…?" Persia tried, and failed, to say.

"Shh," the blonde bombshell pressed a hand to Persia's back for support. "Just take a minute to get your bearings."

Before she could, a stupidly handsome man hurried forward behind the blonde and peered over her shoulder at Persia. Deep concern shaded his blue eyes, the kind of concern someone showered for a loved one, not a total stranger. And he was a stranger to her, yet… something seemed so familiar about him. Blinking the feeling away, she decided he must be a patron at The Lair. She must recognize him from one of her shifts.

"Where am I? Who are you?" she finally managed, reluctantly turning her gaze back to the woman.

"My name's Trina Kincaid and you're in my clinic." She shot a silent warning of some kind to the man, who resembled her. "And this is my brother, Warren Edgecomb. Can you tell me your name?"

"Persia." She rubbed a tender spot on the side of her head. "Persia M-Moonshadow."

"Good," Trina elbowed her overly concerned brother aside. "Look at my finger, Persia. Okay, now follow it without moving your head. Very good. How are you feeling? Dizzy or nauseated?"

"No, but my head hurts like a bitch." Persia did her best not to allow her gaze to flick over Warren. "What the hell happened to me?"

Trina explained as she shone a pen light in Persia's eyes. "I wasn't there, but from what I've been told, you took an elbow to the head, slammed into a wall and then bumped your head against a table. The good news is that it doesn't look like you have a concussion, but your head's going to hurt for a day or two. Now, I'm not set up for, um, injuries like this, so if you want to alleviate any fears, we could take you to a hospital for an MRI—"

Persia managed to wave her hand, dismissing the idea. "God no. Too much trouble. I'm fine, really. As a professional protestor, I've had a helluva lot worse than a headache. One time this cranky construction foreman knocked me on my ass with the bucket of a bulldozer."

Persia thought the story was hilarious, but Warren didn't seem amused in the slightest. In fact, he looked downright furious. "Are you joking? Did that really happen? What's the guy's name and address?"

Trina rolled her eyes and nudged him aside. "Ignore him."

Now that some of her senses were returning to her, Persia took a good look at Trina. "Hey, you seem familiar. Did you stop by Wolf Woods a couple of times last week?"

Trina smiled. "I did. Good memory. Now I'm confident you're not seriously injured. I hear those bulldozers haven't budged an inch since McNish brought them in. Your handiwork?"

Persia beamed. "Not just mine. I've got a team."

"That means yes," Trina chuckled as she checked Persia's pulse. "You're doing a great job."

"Thanks," Persia faltered a bit. Locals often were the hardest to convince when it came to McNish's developments. "Mind if I ask what your deal is? I know why *we're* fighting to keep Wolf Woods wild, but what's at stake for you?"

Warren pushed past Trina, his hands starting to reach for her but then quickly pulling back. His fingers curled into fists, as if he was holding himself back from something, while Trina continued her exam.

"The original settlers of our, uh, village homesteaded the land this side of Wolf Woods. For generations, we've used those woods as an extension of our property, a sort of buffer between the town and us. It's not that we're antisocial and don't want neighbors or anything. It's more that the woods are a local landmark. There's a lot of historical and cultural significance there. Losing the woods would hurt the town as a whole, not just for a bit of public greenspace, but tourists come from all around to search the woods for werewolves."

Persia snorted. She'd researched Wolf Woods and Tremble thoroughly before dragging her caravan there to protest another McNish development. Loonies from around the country flocked to the tiny Georgia town in search of cryptids—chupacabra, Big Foot, and werewolves. The town had cleverly capitalized on the fascination with Wolf Woods, which had turned Tremble into something of a tourist trap. If she'd had the money, she would have loved to spend the night in one of the Lupine Inn's werewolf-themed rooms. As it was, working at The Wolf's Lair Bar & Grille gave her enough of a supernatural vibe, what with all the silly werewolf tchotchkes decorating the place.

"I really can't believe people still believe in all that nonsense." She smiled up at Warren. It felt good, natural. Smiling at him seemed to be what she'd been born to do.

From the corner of her eye, she caught Trina shooting a funny look at her brother, but Persia was too mesmerized by his stormy blue eyes. So mesmerized, she barely noticed another man walking into the clinic from an adjoining room. The man had shaggy, light brown hair and matching hazel eyes with a physique that wouldn't quit. It seemed this village produced a lot of gorgeous people.

"Even so," Trina spoke again, "if Dick McNish gets his way, we'll all suffer from the loss of Wolf Woods."

The man sidled up to Trina and wrapped a protective arm around her shoulders. "McNish is an asshole. He needs to be brought to justice."

"I totally agree," Persia's excitement over finding like-minded people dimmed her pain a little. "You know, if more locals joined our protest, we'd have more footing. Things always go much better when townspeople get involved instead of just looking at us outsiders like we're lunatics. Besides, the more people who protest, the more exposure the issue gets. Strength in numbers and all that."

The trio shared a look that spoke volumes, but Persia didn't have the translation guide. If she had to guess, she would have said they looked intrigued. Better than irritated, so she pushed on.

"Our first step was to set up our base camp and draw some attention with our signs and chants."

"I particularly like 'Down with Dick,'" the man holding onto Trina chimed in. "Name's Max, by the way."

"Nice to meet you, Max. And thanks. That one's mine. Came up with it ages ago."

"So what's your next step?" Warren asked, inching just a little closer to her, which didn't bother her a bit.

Persia grinned up at him, partly from excitement over her plans and partly because she couldn't seem to do anything *except* smile at him. "Building platforms in the trees so they can't be torn down. It's called tree-sitting. We use mountain climbing gear to get way up in the trees to build the platforms, and then we just camp out there to stall development."

Warren's eyes glittered. "Treehouses?" he breathed, clearly excited by the idea.

"Not exactly," Persia laughed at his enthusiasm. "But close enough."

"Count me in. I have access to lumber, tools, and plenty of skilled workmen who'd be thrilled to support the cause."

Persia's heart nearly stuttered to stop, giving new meaning to the quip "Be still my beating heart." Not only was this Warren guy drop-dead gorgeous, but he was eager to join their effort in stopping the development. Taking a beat, she gave him a deep-down assessment. Sandy blond hair, a little darker than his sister's, eyes so blue they pierced her to the core, a lean-yet-muscular swimmer's build, and a desire to save the environment. Or at least stop McNish, anyway. What more could a girl want?

Warren was a true manly man, a far cry from the hacky-sack-loving, pot-smoking hippie guys she tended to hang out with, but the image of him swinging a hammer, shirtless and sweaty with hard work, made her feel tingly in all of her happy places. Meeting his gaze felt a bit like taking a shot of really good tequila, slowly warming every inch of her skin and then soaking through the rest of her.

"How can I turn down an offer like that?" she swung her legs over the side of the gurney and attempted to stand.

As soon as her feet touched the floor, the warmth oozing through her was replaced by a harsh wave of dizziness and she had to press her butt to the gurney to brace herself. Persia was almost certain it was caused by the bump to her head and not the intoxicating scent rolling off Warren.

Almost.

"Whoa," Trina lunged for her patient, but Warren reached Persia first.

His warm hands gently helped her back onto the gurney, and one remained on her shoulder, even after she no longer needed the help. Not that she was complaining.

Trina clucked her tongue. "You probably want to get back to your camp, but it's pretty late and I'd feel a whole lot better if you stayed the night so I can monitor you."

"Good idea," Max dropped a quick kiss on his lady's cheek. "In fact, I made a nice stew for dinner, and there's plenty for a guest."

"Or two," Warren gave his sister a meaningful look.

Trina smirked at him. "Only if you sing for us."

"Uh, no one wants to hear that," he replied, scowling at her and giving her a not-so-subtle head shake.

"Come on, big brother. It's always such a treat." Trina gave Persia a mischievous smile. "He's got a helluva singing voice, when he isn't being greedy with it."

"No," Warren insisted, "she's already got enough of a headache. Last thing she needs is to listen to my caterwauling."

Trina rolled her eyes at her brother's stubbornness and huffed, "Fine."

The back and forth between the siblings warmed Persia's heart. As an only child, she'd never had that bond with another person. She'd had to suffer through her childhood alone. Someone to share the burden might have been nice, but then again, she wouldn't have wished it on her worst enemy.

"Thank you for the offer, but I really do need to get back to work. This might come as a shock but being a professional protestor doesn't pay as much as you'd think."

Warren seemed too concerned to catch her joke. "No, not tonight. Hux feels terrible about what happened and gave you the rest of the night off. With pay."

She'd liked Hux the moment she'd interviewed for the barmaid job, and this little nugget only confirmed her belief he was a good man. That didn't mean she was going to overstay her welcome with her new friends, though.

"That's really nice of him, but I still need to get my Westfalia. It's my home and I'm a little protective of it."

Warren caught her gaze again and any worries she had fled from her mind.

Westfalia? What's that?

Concussion? Who cares?

"No need to worry about your van. It couldn't be anywhere safer than in Hux's parking lot. Trust me on that. I'll drive you down there first thing in the morning. Deal?"

For the first time in her life, Persia had nothing left to protest.

CHAPTER FOUR

WARREN STRETCHED HIS HIND LEGS AND SHOOK HIS FURRY head as the sun peeked over the treetops the next morning. Despite her protests, he'd promised Persia he'd be at the clinic bright and early. Mainly because he knew he'd be sleeping on the steps leading to Trina's clinic. No way was he going to leave his mate alone, not as long as people like McNish were out to destroy their pack. Hell, he'd stay by her side twenty-four-seven, if she'd let him, regardless of what was happening in the world.

It wasn't as if he didn't trust Max and Trina to be in the next room. Well, in truth, he trusted Trina and gave Max the benefit of the doubt since Trina trusted him. She'd probably slice off very important parts of Max if he so much as sniffed in Persia's direction. But he felt more protective of Persia than anything else in his entire life and hadn't been able to force himself away. Even so, a pang of jealousy stabbed his heart when he caught Max's scent surrounding the cabin. It was only natural for a male wolf to want to keep his mate safe, but he no longer wanted jealousy to be part of his life.

Your first reaction is how you were taught to feel, and your second reaction is your true self's response.

That had become Warren's mantra since he'd had a nice long talk a while back with the pack's omega, Cassandra. He'd sought her out not long after his childhood crush, Chloe, had run off with another pack's healer. He'd thought his heart was broken, but Cassandra helped him see it wasn't. Mostly his ego had been bruised. Regardless, he reminded himself of his new mantra on a daily basis, and he found it helped him to be more mindful of the world.

And that wasn't a bad thing.

Warren took his time shifting, still drowsy and stiff from sleeping on hard wood all night. The sun felt good on his bare skin, and he took a moment to bask in it, thanking the heavens for bringing Persia to Tremble. The irony of the situation struck him as he dressed. He really should be thanking Dick McNish. If the asshole hadn't set his sights on Wolf Woods, Persia might never have stepped foot in Tremble and Warren would never have found her.

Not wanting to wake everyone if they still slept, Warren softly rapped a couple of times on the clinic door. He'd learned the hard way not to just barge in anymore. Seeing his sister and her mate going at it *twice* had been enough to teach him that lesson. He was about to turn away when the door swung open. Persia stood there, staring up at him with warmth in her eyes, clearly happy to see him.

Yes!

"Early riser too, huh?" she stepped aside to let him pass.

Trina and Max stood in the pass-through to their cabin, enjoying their morning Earl Grey.

"You could say that," he chuckled, ignoring his sister's smirk.

"Want some tea?" Max struggled to hide his smile at how smitten Warren was with Persia.

"No," Persia answered for him, "we need to get going. Don't need my van getting booted for sitting in the parking lot all night."

Eager to leave the smug atmosphere filling his sister's place, Warren readily agreed and ushered her out the door toward his truck. When he hurried to open the passenger door for her, she gave him a perplexed smile.

"Old fashioned type, huh?"

"Are you telling me you don't like a little chivalry?" Warren quirked an eyebrow at her.

"No way, I'm just not used to it." She climbed into her seat.

Warren knew he shouldn't feel overly proud about making her feel special, but he did. Biting the inside of his cheek, he rounded the truck thinking of everything she'd unwittingly told him in the clearing the day before. If he wanted to woo this woman, he'd have to take his cues wherever he could.

The cab was silent, other than the roar of the engine, as they bumped their way off the mountain and onto the main road leading into Tremble. Persia moved her legs as if to prop them on the dash but stopped short.

"Make yourself comfortable," he told her. "If you haven't noticed, this rattle trap isn't very fancy."

Persia laughed, kicking back as if she owned the beast. Her loud, uninhibited laugh sounded like the daintiest wind chimes, though it was anything but dainty. It suited her so perfectly, and he could tell he'd spend the rest of his life smiling every time she so much as chuckled.

And the fact she was already so comfortable in his presence gave him immense pleasure and a strange sort of joy. The view of her curvy calves when her flowing skirt fell away from them gave him other feelings. Feelings he wouldn't be able to hide if he kept staring at her creamy skin.

Clearing his throat and keeping his eyes trained on the road, he tried to find a safe topic. "Trina gave you the all-clear this morning, I assume."

"Yup, fit as a fiddle. I barely even have a smidge of a headache, just a tender lump." Her fingers fluttered up to her head and gingerly prodded the spot that had come in contact with a table.

"Good to hear. I just hate this was your first impression of Tremble. McNish has really caused a stir. We used to have such a peaceful and friendly community but now..."

"If things hadn't gotten stirred up, I wouldn't be seeing it at all," she pointed out.

"True," Warren chuckled, amused that he'd thought pretty much the same thing.

"Besides, I've seen it happen before. I've followed McNish's delightful path of destruction all over Georgia for... well over a year now." Her sigh held more sadness than Warren would have expected.

"Mind if I ask why you've been on his tail?"

The mood inside the truck darkened as she shot him a sharp glance. "Because what he's doing is beyond criminal. Running people off their ancestral lands? For what? Money? What kind of person does that?"

"An awful one," Warren grimaced.

"McNish is a real piece of work. You'd be shocked how good he is at covering up his activities. I simply can't abide the thought of him destroying so many people's lives and never facing the consequences of that choice."

Her passion intoxicated him. Of course, he wanted to experience a different, more intimate kind of passion with her, but her energy rubbed off on him, exciting him at the thought of stopping McNish.

"And that's why I've dedicated my life to stopping Dick McNish from ruining anyone else's lives."

"Did you see the article about him the other day?"

She shrugged her ambivalence. "It was well-written, but it was only the start of what needs to happen to break through his armor. He's big league, and a measly regional news article won't affect him too much. Now if it had been a national news outlet..."

Warren spent the rest of the ride filling Persia in on the pack's dealings with McNish—what he could, at least—including that Max had been the source for the exposé on McNish.

Pulling into The Lair's barren parking lot, Warren pulled up one spot over from a battered Volkswagen Westfalia van that looked even worse than his old pickup. As she reached for her door handle, he pointed at her.

"Don't move!"

No mate of his would open her own car door, as long as she was okay with it. Judging by the amused smile that turned up the edges of her perfectly plump lips, she was.

"You're the real deal. Aren't you?" She accepted his hand to help her down.

"Not sure what you mean, but I'll take it."

His grin faltered with the nearness of her. Underneath the antiseptic smell from spending the night in Trina's clinic, her true dessert-like scent caught him in the back of the throat. He couldn't even swallow for fear of losing that addictive tickle. Leaning in toward her, Warren couldn't help noticing she didn't pull away. If anything, she leaned in a tiny bit too, craning her neck to stare into his eyes and entrancing him like a siren, luring him in with her mismatched eyes and pure soul.

Persia broke the spell, jerking back with a start and stepping away from the circle of their attraction. Coughing deliberately to buy some time, she flushed scarlet and quickly turned away so he couldn't see. A good start, as far as he was concerned. Moving slowly when his mate was inches away nearly killed him, not to mention brought his wolf so close to the surface he worried he might have sprouted tufts of hair. Hopefully the courting process wouldn't take too long because he wasn't sure he could resist her charms much longer.

"What do you think of Betty?" Persia asked as she pulled out her keys and opened the sliding door to her pale-yellow antiquity.

Blowing out a breath of frustration, he smiled. "Betty? You named your van?"

"Sure, doesn't everyone?" she asked, looking at him like he was the weirdo.

"Uh, no," he chuckled as he peered inside.

Threadbare wasn't a strong enough term to describe the front seats. Chewed up and spit out would have been more like it. The original tan- and brown-striped tweed had worn down into strips, allowing the cushioning underneath to peek through. A badly cut hunk of orange shag carpet lay on the floor behind the seats where a built-in beige-and-brown cabinet served as a tiny kitchenette. Unlit twinkle lights hung along the ceiling, which had latches that allowed the whole thing to tilt up to offer some head room. A large faded flag reading *Free Tibet!* lay draped over the back seat. Persia pushed a foot stool-looking box with a matching seat cushion out of the way, grimacing an apology at him.

"What?" he asked, clueless.

"That's the Portapotty. Sorry."

Warren's home, a small cabin just inside the woods near the pack house, wasn't overly large, but it was a mansion compared to Persia's camper van. Camping for a few days in such a contraption would be one thing, but living out of one was something entirely different.

"You... *live* in this? For real?"

She must have caught his look of disbelief and snorted. "Lots of people have to live in their cars or worse these days, Warren. Way I see it, I'm living in the lap of luxury, compared to them. Besides, it doesn't make sense to pay rent on an apartment when I travel so much."

He grunted noncommittally, unwilling to put words to the way he felt about her living in such an insecure space. She *deserved* to live in a mansion with all the luxurious trappings—not that he could give that to her, but compared to a van, his cabin might actually *seem* like one.

"Looks like the perfect size for one person," he did his best not to put any emphasis on "one." The funny look she gave him said he failed.

After the "tour" of her van, Persia awkwardly glanced at him, then the ground, then the sky. "Well, um, thanks for the ride." She spoke quietly.

That was his cue to leave, but he'd be damned if he'd let her park this janky rig off the side of the road. A serial killer could stumble upon her, or even worse, she might be tempted to chill with her ex again. Uh-uh, no way. But he'd have to handle it delicately, so he didn't scare her off.

"You know, a friend of mine is a local cop, and he told me yesterday that they're going to ramp up patrols around Wolf Woods to make sure no one's camping there. Might not be the best idea for you to park at the entrance like you've been doing."

Persia's face crumpled into a frown. "Oh."

She glanced around, as if trying to determine whether living in Hux's parking lot might be an option. Luckily Warren had an alternative that *wasn't* his house, which he had a feeling she wouldn't like at this stage of their relationship.

"I'm sure Trina wouldn't mind if you parked outside her place. You and your van would be totally safe and out of reach from the local police."

"You think?" she asked, her distracting eyes lighting up with hope.

"I know."

The sun glinted off her dazzling smile, and oh god, those dimples. "Back to Trina's!"

CHAPTER FIVE

An hour or so later, Warren proudly pulled into the parking area in front of Wolf Woods with Persia in the passenger seat of his truck. This time her excitement got the better of her and she didn't wait for him to open her door. It was bound to happen from time to time, but he was determined to keep trying until it became habit. Besides, her excitement was warranted. The bed of his truck overflowed with enough lumber and tools to build at least a couple of treehouses, and more was on the way.

"Are you sure about this?" Persia questioned him for the third time. She'd worried about the cost of all the building materials and using up all of his supplies.

"Too late now, don't you think?" He winked, which sent a flush of pink to her cheeks. "Besides, there's more coming."

The rest of the protestors laid down their signs and wandered over, curious and wary, until they spotted Persia. The skinny kid from the tarp-tent approached but lurched to a stop at Warren's pointed glare. Warren had caught enough of a whiff to know he was Persia's most recent ex, Leaf. *Leaf!* The kid spun on his heel and returned to his spot under the McNish billboard. Maybe he wasn't so dumb after all.

"I… *we* can't thank you enough," Persia was saying as she pulled down the tailgate.

"Southern hospitality, Red," he replied, brushing up against her as he reached for a sheet of plywood.

She stiffened against the touch and the scent of her desire hit Warren like a grenade. *Yes!* She wanted him just as much as he wanted her. Hopefully she would forget about her vow to shun men and give in to her primal needs. Soon.

"Okay, we'll go with that, country boy," she whispered and then moved away far too quickly.

A crowd gathered around the truck and Persia startled him by clapping loudly as she turned to face her friends. "Alright, everyone, listen up! This is my friend Warren. He's doing us a big favor by offering up a load of lumber and tools for our cause. He's also called in some backup to help. You know what that means—we're getting some tree-sitting platforms set up today! I want every able pair of hands we've got working on the platforms. If you don't know how to build, help move materials. Let's go!"

To his surprise, the crowd immediately obeyed Persia's orders, lining up to help unload the truck. That such a tiny woman could command so many people so skillfully impressed him. But as soon as the bed was empty, a handful of the younger protestors wandered away, trying to melt into the woods so they wouldn't have to do more manual labor. At least the older ones—mid-twenties, tops—tried to figure out which was the working end of a hammer.

By then a few more trucks loaded down with supplies had arrived, and out tumbled two of his pack mates per truck. Persia rounded up the lazy stragglers and assigned them to different duties, as if she'd done so many times before. From the sounds of it, she had.

The guys he'd borrowed from Zeke's construction company worked with their assigned teams of protestors, a few shooting him dirty looks for roping them into teaching basic carpentry. They could grumble all they liked, but it was for a good cause. The pack could certainly survive without access to Wolf Woods, but after McNish's hired hunters had shot poor Little Hux, the seven-year-old son of Hux Davenport, when he was in his wolf form, the Soren pack had considered themselves at war.

Warren didn't follow Persia around as she organized everyone, but he also never let her out of his sight. She moved with an agility that belied her stature, which got him thinking about how flexible she might be. A flash of an image of her with her knees up near her ears brought on a coughing fit he couldn't control. It was better than walking around the group with a raging hard-on, but just barely. Turning back to his pile of supplies, he discovered Persia strapping a tool belt around her waist and giving him a big thumbs-up.

"Ready?" She was so full of energy and enthusiasm.

Strapping on his own tool belt and hefting a pile of two-by-fours onto his shoulder, he jerked his head toward the trees. "After you."

Warren enjoyed following her into the woods as she looked for the perfect tree for her treehouse. About a hundred yards in, she found it. It was a sturdy old sycamore that had plenty of space in its branches for a platform. Maybe not a big one, but it would be temporary at best anyway.

"Ooh, she's perfect," Persia crooned as she gazed up at the gnarled branches and lush canopy. "What do you think?"

"Perfect," he agreed, his eyes never leaving her lush curves and fiery hair.

She must have heard something in his tone because she turned a curious blue eye on him. Whatever she saw on his face—pure, unadulterated lust, most likely—sent an adorable pink flush high on her cheeks, and she turned back to the tree quickly.

"Let's get started." She grabbed a two-by-four and then stood there, looking at it with no idea what to do next.

Working side by side with his mate was Warren's idea of heaven. Persia took instruction well and caught on quickly, almost as if she'd worked on job sites a time or two in her life. Pretty soon she didn't even need any direction from him. As the other teams searched for their own trees, Warren and Persia had already found a rhythm.

Generators and power tools found their way to the general area the protestors were building in, and then construction really got underway. Climbing the tree freestyle, he wrapped a few climbing ropes over a thick, sturdy limb and sent the bitter ends down to Persia to set up a lift system using pulleys to haul up the wood and themselves. Without hesitation, Persia strapped herself into a climbing harness, clipped into the rope, and pulled herself up with the pulleys. A couple of guys remained on the ground to send up their supplies.

"Phew, hot up here," Warren commented as he pulled his shirt over his head.

"Uh huh," she murmured absently, which drew his attention. Persia stood with a hammer hanging loosely from her hand as she stared at his bare chest.

"You seem to know your way around a hammer," Warren teased, giving her a wink as she shook herself back to reality.

"Don't get any ideas," she laughed, settling onto a branch. "I might know what to do with a hammer and handsaw, but that's about the limit of my skills."

Warren grabbed the first piece of plywood and she helped stabilize it between their two branches. "Was it a gig between protests?" he asked as he started hammering the wood down.

Her silence caught his attention, and when he glanced her way, she was busy looking at the spot she was holding onto. "I worked during the summers when I was at school."

"Oh? What did you study?"

"Poly sci as an undergrad and then law."

"Law?" He nearly dropped the hammer. "Damn, I knew you were smart, but I didn't realize we had a lawyer on our hands."

"Environmental law," she spoke casually, as if it were no big deal and not a huge accomplishment that Warren felt secondhand pride for. "You could say this kind of thing is in my blood, y'know?"

"A woman who knows what she wants. Gotta appreciate that. "

"You seem to appreciate a lot about me."

Her expression held a promise and a warning, and Warren couldn't decide which excited him more. Still, he'd been trying to play it cool with her, but she'd sniffed him out. Not above flirting with his own mate—even if she didn't know it yet—he let his lips twist up into a slow, seductive smile.

"What's not to appreciate?"

Heat and attraction vibrated between them, filling the air high up in the tree with tension. As if the risk of falling to their deaths wasn't enough already. Tree sex would definitely be risky, but Warren was up for it if Persia was. Before he could figure out a way to broach the subject without sounding like a total perv, she got to work nailing down her side of the platform. Then she sang.

It was a pop song, filled with angst and love and longing. Something he'd heard before but couldn't place. It was old, he knew that much, but as a country music fan, he couldn't identify it. Of course, it could have been the delivery. Persia's rendition was badly off-key and almost painful to listen to. And he loved it.

"What?" she asked, when she caught him grinning at her.

"Nothing. What song is that?"

"*Endless Love*. Why don't you join me? You *have* to know *Endless Love*. It's a classic."

Nothing would have pleased him more than to join her in endless love, but she was probably talking about the song, not their future together.

"Nah, no one wants to hear that." He pushed another board in place. "Besides, I like the way you sing it better. In fact, I wouldn't mind hearing more. Maybe a private concert somewhere quieter?"

He lifted a suggestive brow at her, at which she rolled her eyes with the drama of a soap opera actress.

"Jeesh, didn't your daddy ever teach you to buy a girl some flowers before propositioning her?"

Damn, wrong move. He shrugged, trying his best to cover up his sad attempt at seduction, and blurted out the first thing that came to his mind.

"You'll have to pick your own flowers. Too frou frou for me."

He immediately regretted it. If Persia wanted flowers, he'd pick a whole hillside worth, just to get to see her dimples again. He'd only wanted to ease any worry she had about him, not turn her off him completely. *Idiot!*

"Nice," she drawled, her tone implying she thought otherwise. He'd really stepped in it this time.

They worked in silence after that. He tried to crack a couple of jokes, but she couldn't even manage enough of a smirk to activate her dimples.

"Well, this thing looks pretty sturdy." She climbed into her harness again. "Guess it's about time for some lunch."

Hope flared in Warren's chest that she might invite him to eat with her, but his rude comment had obviously made her think better of *that.*

"Think I'm gonna slip off and grab some frou frou lunch in my van, maybe take a walk and pick myself some flowers." She began lowering herself to the ground. Before her head disappeared below the platform, she caught his gaze. "Alone."

Good god, this woman frustrated him! The scent of her desire clouded his senses, but he had enough of his faculties to know her running off like that wasn't the way it was supposed to work. Watching every move as she lowered herself down the tree like an expert, Warren knew what he had to do. It wasn't his first choice, but he'd screwed that up royally. Time to pull out the big guns.

"She might not like me very much, but I know who she *does* like."

CHAPTER SIX

"PERSIA, YOU DIDN'T SAY ANYTHING ABOUT DOING construction work when you recruited me for this gig," a rail-thin young brunette named Joy whined.

Her boyfriend, Rustle—not Russell, but *Rustle*—joined her, oh-so-eloquently agreeing. "Yeah."

Pretty soon Persia was surrounded by the group she led, some complaining about physical labor, some wanting to know the best tree to build in, and a couple bitching about hurting the trees by pounding nails into them. Normally, she wouldn't have minded being bombarded with questions and gripes, but her nerves were already on a razor-thin edge. Especially after being in such close proximity to a certain sweaty, impeccably ripped, handsome as hell redneck. It was all she could do to hold her temper at bay.

It took a good fifteen minutes to hear everyone's concerns, but Persia counted herself lucky they hadn't insisted on a peace circle, where they all stood around holding hands and voicing any and every thought that came to them. They were good people—for the most part—but damn, they could be exhausting. As most of them wandered off, Leaf hovered around the perimeter, shooting sly glances her way.

"What is it, Leaf?" She released an annoyed sigh. The woods were calling to her, and the thought of having Leaf beg her take him back got on her last nerve.

"You, uh, never came back last night," he ventured, his tone soft and maybe a little sad.

She didn't want to hurt him, but she didn't dare show any vulnerability or he'd try to take advantage, as he always did. "Very astute."

She turned on her heel and headed for the woods. The sandwich she'd left in Warren's truck could wait till she was calmer. She wasn't about to stand there and let her ex-boyfriend shame her for living her life the way she saw fit, even though she'd spent the night in a clinic rather than a certain someone's bed.

"Were you with that guy?"

She stumbled slightly and looked at the ground, pretending to search for the root that had jumped out to trip her. Glancing back, she shot Leaf a dark stare.

"What I do, and with whom I do it, are none of your business, Leaf. Now if you'll excuse me..."

Leaf snorted, a hateful sound she'd never heard come from him before. "You're fucking him. Aren't you?"

This time Persia stopped cold, darting a quick glance up her tree—no sign of Warren. He must have slipped past as she dealt with the mob, thank goodness. Having him hear Leaf's accusation would have killed her with embarrassment.

She slowly turned her fiery glare on Leaf. He didn't even wince. Instead he jammed his fists on his hips in a defiant move. A few of the other protestors leaned toward them, trying to hear the latest juicy gossip.

"Not that it's your business—" she skimmed her gaze across the others "—or *any of yours,* but no. I'm not fucking him."

If they'd asked if she *wanted* to, she'd have a hard time lying because her fair skin would turn beet red, revealing her true feelings. Stupid passion skin!

"He's a guy who has a vested interest in keeping Wolf Woods wild, just like us. He and his friends wanted to help, so I invited them to join us. They're good people and we're lucky to have them. Not only are they doing most of the work y'all should be doing, but it's always best to have locals on our side. Don't you think?"

Leaf glowered and a few others exchanged skeptical looks, but no one uttered a word. Persia didn't waste the chance to get the hell out of there. The woods enveloped her quickly and before long she could breathe again. Slowing to an easy stroll, she let the tensions of the past twenty-four hours melt from her shoulders. The bump on her head was still tender, but other than that, she felt fine.

More than fine.

Something about Warren called to her, just like nature. She'd always felt whole walking in the woods, sitting on a pristine beach, or hiking up a magnificent hillside. Like a missing part of her had finally been found. Inexplicably, Warren had a similar effect on her, only with the added delight of sexual tension.

Recalling the way he manhandled that sheet of plywood turned her fifty shades of tingly. When he'd tugged his shirt over his head, she'd nearly tumbled out of the tree ass over teakettle. Taut, flat muscles spread across his chest and down his belly. Not bulging muscles like a bodybuilder's, more like a swimmer's or a guy who'd achieved such magnificence through physical labor instead of a gym.

"Get a grip, Persia," she snarled at herself.

After all of her self-righteous declarations about being done with men, here she was fantasizing about a brawny good ol' boy she'd just met. The last thing she needed was a distraction, especially in the form of a sexy country boy who knew how to handle his tools. Definitely not at such a pivotal point in the protest against McNish. It was too much of a risk.

She'd been playing her protest game long enough to know better than to let a couple of minor victories make her complacent. Men like Dick McNish prided themselves on operating above the law. He'd wait and watch for her to lose her edge. The group needed to keep their eyes on the prize. Her people, as nice as most of them were, needed her to keep up the momentum and energy. They all looked to her for guidance and leadership

It was a lot of responsibility, which she generally relished. She was a born leader, one of the few benefits of her schooling, but sometimes it weighed her down. That was when she found some way to commune with Mother Nature. No matter the setting, she always felt small in a way that comforted and inspired her. Like she was a tiny piece of a massive, beautiful jigsaw puzzle.

Taking her familiar route, Persia broke through the dense underbrush and into her favorite clearing. To her delight, the same sandy-furred wolf sat in the center, his intelligent blue eyes tracking her every move as he panted and wagged his fluffy tail. What were the odds a human woman and a wild wolf would be in the same exact spot on two different days? Astronomical, which planted the completely illogical seed that the wolf had been waiting for her, as if he knew she was on her way. It was stupid, utterly ridiculous, but she couldn't shake the feeling.

"Hi, handsome." She grinned broadly as she walked toward him. Too bad the charm of dimples were lost on animals.

He met her halfway, pressing the side of his huge body against her legs. She patted his soft head, but he continued pushing against her legs, as if wanting something from her.

"What is it?" She only understood what he wanted when he pushed what should have been a terrifyingly huge muzzle against the backs of her knees, nearly toppling her over. "Okay, okay," she laughed and sat on the bed of grass.

A groan of satisfaction rumbled out of the beast as he laid his head in her lap and looked up at her with big puppy dog eyes. Persia ran her fingers across his snout and along his cheeks, ending up with her fingers wrapped around the softest fur she'd ever felt.

"Oh, you like that, don't you? Me too."

The wolf rolled onto his side, totally blissed out by her attention. Unafraid, Persia planted one hand on the other side of his body and leaned against his bulk. He was like a giant, living body pillow, and after the last couple of days, the physical contact soothed her.

"This is really weird. You know that, right? I mean, it's almost as if you understand me. Which would be a first," she snorted and then sighed. "Well, except maybe that sexy construction guy."

The wolf slapped his tail to the ground and rolled onto his back underneath her arm, his forepaws limp above his chest, looking for the world like he was begging. Persia tucked a red curl behind her ear and smiled down at him.

"Only… what kind of guy refuses to buy a lady flowers when he knows she likes them? That's kinda shitty, right? Selfish, too." The attitude Warren had given her about flowers—not that she expected any from him in the first place—seemed contradictory to his kind and generous personality. "Good thing I'm not interested in dating or that might have hurt my feelings."

Her friend whined softly and bent his head far enough to lick her hand a few times until she acquiesced and petted him.

"Besides, I have to stay strong. Can't get distracted, even if he *is* very distracting. I'm here to effect real change, my friend, not hook up with the local boys. I want to keep these woods around for creatures like you, as well as the locals who use them for recreation. Condos can be built anywhere, but once these woods are gone, they're gone forever. I need to focus on stopping Dick McNish and nothing else."

She'd almost convinced herself, but Warren's smile flickered in her brain, sending sparkles and fireworks bouncing along her nerves.

"It's a lot to take on, I know, but no one out there knows McNish like I do. I've studied him for so long. I know all of his strengths, weaknesses, and tricks he uses to turn those weaknesses in his favor. I've tracked his path of destruction all over the state, but no matter how hard I try to get people to see him for what he really is—a cold, greedy monster—he keeps getting away with his atrocities. No one seems to understand, but I do. That's why I can't let it go or do something else that might be productive. If I don't at least *try* to stop him, nobody else will."

The bushes she'd pushed through to enter the clearing rustled loudly. Something big was coming, and before Persia could react, the wolf had leapt to his feet and stepped in front of her, as if to protect her. His head dropped threateningly low, and every muscle under his fur rippled with tension. Even the darker stripe along his spine had risen, and the snarl coming from deep inside him put her even more on edge.

"What is it, boy?" she murmured as she jumped to her feet, vaguely aware she sounded like a character out of *Lassie*.

Before she could really get frightened, a man and woman emerged from the tree line—a pair of lovers out for a romantic stroll. It would have been downright adorable, if a very large, very angry wolf wasn't ready to pounce on them like they were his next meal. Persia was about to lunge for him, to hold him back, even if it meant she would be his next target. Before she could, though, the wolf dropped to his haunches at her side and let out a soft, "Rumph."

"Please don't be afraid," she called out, even though the couple looked more amused than anything. "He's actually really nice."

The man, a tall, handsome fellow with brown hair that glimmered with copper glints in the sunlight, shot his companion a smirk as they approached. "Oh, we know. We've seen him around."

"You have?" Suddenly Persia didn't feel quite so special anymore. It was silly, but she'd rather enjoyed the fantasy she'd somehow tamed a wild animal.

"A time or two," the woman spoke. She was almost as tall as her fella and nearly as muscled, as evidenced by her shorts and tank top. Her black hair was pulled into a tight ponytail that highlighted her high, tawny cheekbones and keen dark eyes.

"Sorry if we, um, interrupted you." The man was clearly trying not to smile. "I'm Zeke Soren."

"Hi, Zeke. I'm Persia Moonshadow." She extended her arm for a handshake, which she repeated with his wife, who he introduced as Valerie.

"I'm the, uh, mayor of our little village just up the road. I think you've met Max and Trina, as well as her brother Warren."

Persia laughed. "Wow, word sure spreads fast out in the country. "

"We all keep an eye on each other," Zeke confirmed.

"Then you must also know I'm sort of the ringleader of the protest against the McNish Development Corporation."

"Trust me," Valerie's eyes turned stormy, "we know more about Dick McNish than we want to."

"Then just think of me as his natural enemy," Persia replied, smiling proudly. She loved finding kindred spirits —or at least ones with shared enemies. Her fingers found their way to the wolf's head and buried deeply into his thick fur.

Zeke tilted his head as if he was assessing her. "We also heard you're a lawyer. That true?"

When folks found out she was a lawyer, they often peppered her with questions about things she knew little about, so she was always hesitant to share that detail about herself. But Valerie and Zeke seemed savvy enough to not ask how to sue their great-step-uncle's estate for not putting them in his will.

"Yeah."

"Great," Zeke brightened. "We were wondering, since we're on the same side and all, if you could file some kind of injunction against McNish or something?"

Persia's shoulders slumped and a defeated sigh escaped her. "I really wish I could. I've tried time and again, but he covers his bases too well. So well I have yet to find a solid legal reason that a judge wouldn't laugh me out of court, even if he wasn't on McNish's payroll."

The pair exchanged one of those psychic looks couples develop over years and years together, though they looked awfully young to have been together that long.

"Actually, we might be able to help on that front," Valerie offered. "What if we had evidence that an endangered species of stink beetle inhabits Wolf Woods? Think that would do the trick?"

Persia's jaw nearly dropped to the ground and her eyes grew wide. As her heart sped up, her fingers clutched the wolf's fur. But instead of whining in complaint, the beast sort of hummed with excitement, as if he either felt her emotions or understood what was happening. Obviously, it was the former, but it certainly felt like the latter.

"Oh my god, that would be *huge!* Of course, I'd need to confirm their existence, maybe call an entomologist I know, but if what you're saying is true, that might actually work. Courts tend to err on the side of caution when the continuing existence of an entire species is at stake."

"And we've come up with an alternate plan we think McNish might go for, if he's faced with this kind of challenge," Zeke added. "We're hoping you'll attend a meeting with us later to pitch the plan to him."

Persia's stomach knotted and a cold sweat broke out on her forehead. Face to face with Dick McNish again. She'd done everything in her power to avoid even looking at the man for the last couple of years, and while she'd rather chew off her own arm than go to a meeting with him, the locals who'd trusted her enough to join forces needed her.

"Present a united front, huh?" she mused, buying time to make a decision. "Will that Warren guy be there? You know who I'm talking about?"

The pair beamed at each other. "We do."

"He's nice and all, but between you and me, he's a little pushy for my taste."

Zeke pinched his nose and coughed into his hand, giving Persia the distinct impression he struggled not to laugh.

Valerie answered for them both. "That's going to be tough because he's actually the one who came up with the plan."

"Really?" Persia balked. "I didn't think he had much more going on than a pretty face and a rockin' bod."

It was Valerie's turn to hide her amusement while Zeke took over the speaking role. "If it makes any difference, I personally guarantee he will be on his best behavior. And I think you'll have a better impression of him afterward. So, will you come?"

As much as she wanted to say no, she couldn't back out. Her passion for the world they lived in overpowered her desire to avoid looking into Dick McNish's cold, dead eyes again. Looking up to face Zeke, she caught him glaring at her wolf before quickly meeting her gaze. Weird, but everything about this protest had been weird.

"Okay, I'll do it."

CHAPTER SEVEN

From the back seat of Zeke's SUV, Warren glared out the window. The day had started so beautifully by spending time with his mate, but then Zeke and Val just had to come along and spoil everything. He chanced a glance at them, and sure enough, they were *still* smirking. Crossing his arms in a huff, he turned back to the window. A view of kudzu was a million times better than their smug asses.

"So, how long are you planning on trying to melt her heart as a wolf?" Zeke asked the question, ending on a snicker.

"Don't," Warren grunted.

"Gonna ask her for a *bone* on your first date? Get it? *Bone?*"

"Does Val still feed you kibble?" Warren snapped. "Oh yeah, I heard *all* about it."

"Fucking Levi," Zeke growled, scowling at the road while Val barked out a laugh.

The kibble incident after their first meeting would live forever in infamy, though Warren had convinced Levi, who'd witnessed the whole thing and couldn't wait to share it, to never tell another soul or Zeke might have his head on a stick. Still, he wasn't above using the little nugget to his own advantage.

"Look, man, I'm on your side," Zeke scratched at the scruff on his face. "All I'm saying is the lady may think wolves are cute and fluffy, but how's she supposed to fall in love with you? You're barking up the wrong tree, my friend."

"He's barking up the right tree," Val corrected. "The problem is the fact he's *barking*."

"Fuck my life," Warren groaned under his breath and pressed his hot forehead to the cool glass. "I get it. I'm just taking what I can get as far as spending time with her goes. You heard her. She doesn't even *like* me all that much. How the hell am I supposed to convince her she's my mate?"

Val turned in the passenger seat to face him. "First of all, stop thinking in terms of 'your mate.' She has no idea what that means. It will fuck with her mind, and I say that as someone who was in her shoes not so long ago. Wait—" she looked over at her mate "—are Birkenstocks shoes or sandals?"

Zeke slapped the steering wheel as he chortled. "They're an abomination, if you ask me."

Val smiled and rolled her eyes. "Whatever. My point is that it took me a while to wrap my head around the whole shifter thing in general when Chloe explained it to me back in college. Otherwise, I would have totally flipped my shit when I met Zeke."

"What do you suggest then?" Warren was desperate for any scrap of advice that would result in Persia falling head over heels for him.

"I dunno. Ease her into it. Go slowly. Treat her with respect. Maybe learn her real name, because... come on, *Moonshadow?*"

That set Zeke on another laughing fit. Ignoring his alpha, as well as Val's suggestion, Warren leaned forward. "How did you react when Chloe told you?"

"Um, about the same way you would if you caught your roommate turning into a mermaid and flopping around on the floor."

Warren waved away the analogy. "But how did she *tell* you?"

"I don't recall the dirty details. I accidentally saw her shift and she sat me down to explain it all."

"What kind of questions did you ask her?"

Val and Zeke shared a grim look, and Warren knew exactly what they were thinking at each other. *Poor bastard.* He didn't care. He needed hope, and at that moment, Val was his best chance.

"I gotta be honest, Warren. The only big question I had was how she got anything done when she was able to lick her own pussy as a wolf."

Zeke nearly drove them into a ditch from laughing so hard.

Warren was far from amused. "Come on, you guys. I'm flying blind here. Tell me this. How long did it take for you to, as you said, wrap your head around it?"

"I don't really remember," Val shrugged. "A week? Maybe as long as six months to really accept it? Hard to say, it was so long ago."

"Six *months*! I really care about this woman, but I don't want to scare her so badly she winds up in a mental hospital. Help me out."

"Hey, I'd bet good money she already believes in aliens and ghosts." Val flashed him another grin. "You've got that going for you. Maybe it won't be such a leap."

"Listen, Warren," Zeke chimed in, "I'm just giving you shit. You're a really good guy. You just gotta take it slowly and let her get to know the real you, not just the meathead.

But don't take it too slowly or she'll think you're not interested. Just the perfect amount of slow."

Warren rolled his eyes and slumped back into his seat. "Right. Great. Thanks for nothing."

The big rig rumbled into the McNish Development Corporation's Tremble headquarters. Everyone in the pack had come to hate the site of the shiny new construction trailer, mostly because it served as a highly visible reminder that McNish wasn't going anywhere.

As they climbed out of the SUV, a familiar face caught Warren's eye. And judging by the way Zeke's hands clenched into tight fists, his alpha had spotted the man, too. Randy Leeper, the asshole who'd shot Little Hux's arm with his hunting rifle and nearly killed Max, happened to be McNish's head wolf hunter. He even wore the camo to prove it, though his hunting rifle was nowhere to be seen. He *was* cupping something in his hands, but it was too small to see.

Leeper looked up as they approached and smiled broadly, as if welcoming old friends, and then started toward them. Zeke stopped in his tracks, tensing and getting a little furry around the collar. This was not the time to get into a brawl in the parking lot, but before Warren could hold Zeke back from ripping out Leeper's throat, Val stepped in front of her mate.

As former military, Val followed the line of command to the letter. Her habit to protect her superior officers was deeply engrained. Even though Zeke was also her mate, he was the alpha of the pack, and she saw it as her duty to be his first line of defense. Within the confines of their relationship, they were equals, but where the pack was concerned, Zeke was the leader and he needed to remain safe. Warren stepped up just behind Val, in case something bad went down.

The closer Leeper got, the less it seemed he wanted a fight. He had a sort of dreamy look on his face and almost floated toward them. Instead of punching her, he pulled Val into a classic one-armed, Southern-style side hug.

Warren glanced back to see Zeke seething at the sight of a strange man—an enemy to boot—touching his mate, but before he could shift and tear the asshole to pieces, Leeper turned to Zeke and repeated the hug. When he grabbed Warren for a hug, they all looked at each other in confusion. Was it some kind of subversive tactic? The hunters had tried that once, but Valerie had pointed it out so they wouldn't get sucked in. But this…this was off-the-charts weird.

"Look!" Randy began with the enthusiasm of a child, releasing Warren and holding out his hand.

Warren was almost afraid to look. It would have been right up Randy's alley to have something deadly that would kill them all in an instant. But one glance stunned Warren more than the hugs.

Three tiny yellow flowers lay on his big, calloused palm. One by one, he passed a flower to each of them, smiling as if he'd just handed over the Crown Jewels.

"Ain't they purty?" His voice was filled with wonder. "Imma go find more."

Without so much as another look at them, he spun around and walked away with a spring in his step that could almost have been mistaken for skipping. They watched him for a long moment before Val whispered, "What the fuck was *that*?"

"Remember, Cassandra said she put a spell on him to keep him from hunting wolves," Zeke murmured under his breath, staring after the guy. "Maybe that seed she planted went a little deeper than she expected."

"As long as it keeps him off pack lands, I'm happy," Warren muttered and the others agreed with solemn nods.

"Don't get too comfortable," Val warned. "It could just as easily be some kind of ruse to make us lower our guards."

Dropping the flowers in the dirt, the trio stomped up the steps to the trailer's door, Zeke in the lead. He threw the door open with relish, letting it slam against the side of the trailer—and hopefully marring its shiny exterior. A middle-aged woman stood and smiled at them.

"Good afternoon." Her tone was perfectly pleasant, though a flicker of wariness sparked in her eyes. "You must be the, um, homesteaders. Please, have a seat around the conference table."

Zeke ignored her outstretched arm pointing toward the table and glowered at her. "Where's Dick?"

She pressed her lips together at his rudeness. "Mr. McNish will be here shortly. Now, if you'll just—"

Zeke held up a hand. "That's alright, ma'am. We'll wait for our attorney to arrive."

The woman stiffened and then nodded tersely and left them alone in the trailer. The space was set up with a handful of desks for various workers, a small snack station with a coffee maker, and an artist's renderings of the proposed condos McNish wanted to build in Wolf Woods. They looked pretty much like every other condo ever built—sterile and tightly controlled. Nothing like the lush wildness of the woods.

The putt-putt-putt of a small diesel engine sputtering into the parking lot set Warren's heart pounding. She'd arrived. Any second now, his mate would walk through the door and the razor's edge of frustration he'd been tiptoeing along since lunch would level out and give him firmer footing.

He sensed Persia's tension before she even opened the door. Smiling just a little too brightly, she greeted everyone as she breezed in like nothing troubled her. Warren wasn't a fashionista, but the outfit she'd changed into looked vintage. Her calf-length flowing floral skirt ended in vibrant pink-and-yellow striped knee-high socks tucked into scuffed brown leather clogs. Her purple peasant blouse offered a delicious peek at her shoulders, and Warren suddenly found himself fantasizing about kissing that creamy, soft neck as far as the fabric would allow. Shaking the image from his head—for the moment—he couldn't stop himself from smiling at her unique style. Probably not what one would expect from a lawyer, but somehow, she pulled it off flawlessly.

Persia brushed past him, her sweet candy scent filling his nostrils as she ignored him and took a seat near the head of the table. Everyone followed suit, Warren settling directly across from her. He wanted to be close, but not scare her off. He also wanted a good view of her face, not just because it was the loveliest he'd ever seen, but maybe he could pick up clues about what was bothering her if he could watch her expressions.

The trouble was she barely lifted her head from the papers she pulled out of her soft-sided briefcase, almost as if she was avoiding his gaze. The uneasy silence grew more uncomfortable as she shuffled through some files and organized them neatly in front of her. Something was definitely eating at her. He wanted to ask what. He wanted to take her in his arms and comfort her. Tell her that whatever she was nervous about would work out just fine, as long as they were together. But she wasn't ready. He knew that and hated it.

When she finally lifted her face and graced him with her stunning bi-colored eyes, Warren thought he'd died and gone to heaven. "Zeke and Val tell me this was all your idea."

All he could manage was a weak nod.

"Well," she continued, stiffening her back until it was ramrod straight, "good job. This is just the kind of thing that could save Wolf Woods."

Her tone remained neutral, as if giving him a compliment was the hardest thing for her to do, yet Warren felt as if he'd just won an Academy Award, or even better, a Nobel Peace Prize. Heat flooded his face and he scratched behind his left ear in his discomfort.

"Um, thanks. Just, you know, doing my part."

Persia laid down the folder she'd been holding and leaned in toward him, her gaze locking onto his and not letting him go. Whatever was going on inside her had nothing—or at least almost nothing—to do with him, that much he could sense from her.

"No, Warren. I really mean it. The plan you put together… It's good. Really good. You gave us some serious firepower, and you should be proud of yourself."

The wall in her gaze began crumbling. Brick by brick, the distance she'd put between them fell away, revealing a yearning Warren had hoped for. In her blue right eye, he saw a life of love and laughter lasting until they were old, wrinkled and hobbled. In her brown left eye, he saw the cutest curly-haired pups growing into solid members of the pack and having pups of their own. Emotion burned the backs of his eyes as he searched hers to ensure it was real, but before he could, footsteps sounded on the metal staircase leading to the trailer door.

And the wall slammed back up.

Warren blinked in confusion, not only at the abrupt change, but at the anxiety wafting off her in plumes. But he didn't have time to puzzle it out. McNish was on his way so he had to bury his troubles, just as she did. When the door opened and McNish strolled in, Persia straightened and returned her eyes to her files.

"Apologies for my tardiness." He oozed dishonesty and arrogance. He wasn't the least bit sorry. More than likely, his late arrival had been a deliberate attempt to throw them off their game. To add insult to injury, he didn't even bother looking at them as he approached the table. He was too engrossed in his phone, or at least he pretended to be.

Glancing up briefly, he found Zeke and tipped his head. The alpha glowered, unable to rein in his hatred for the man who was responsible for nearly killing two members of the Soren pack. Val's expression remained as stony and impassive as ever, but Warren sensed her rage simmering just under the surface. If the man so much as looked at Zeke the wrong way, she'd be on him like a tiger on an injured wildebeest. McNish barely skimmed past Warren, dismissing him as irrelevant, and then his gaze landed on Persia.

Blinking in surprise, McNish lowered his phone and stared at her while she lifted her chin defiantly and stared right back. Warren had only had a few interactions with the man, but he never would have imagined McNish would ever reveal his true feelings about anything. Yet it didn't take a mind reader to see McNish's shock.

"Oh," McNish half-laughed, half-choked out. "Hi, princess."

Without missing a beat, Persia spoke the last words Warren ever expected.

"Hi, Daddy."

CHAPTER EIGHT

THE TENSION IN THE TRAILER INTENSIFIED SO MUCH LEAF'S favorite potato starch-based spork could have sliced it. Every cell in Persia's body flipped into defense mode, as her body did so often when confronted with such insane levels of awkwardness. Still, she refused to look away from her father first. Taking a page from his book, she wouldn't let her true feelings show, no matter how difficult. Not only for the sake of preserving her reputation with her new friends, but also with her father. As twisted as his ethics were, he was shrewd. He knew which buttons of hers to push because he'd installed them when she was just a child. But she hadn't been his sweet little princess for a very long time.

Looking up at the old man he'd become, Persia didn't see a doting father. She saw trouble. She saw her enemy. She saw red. The years-long battle between them had yet to be settled and probably never would. They were too different *and* too similar. Stubborn, headstrong, relentless. They'd stop at nothing to win, but for very different reasons. Persia fought for the betterment of the planet. Her life centered around self-sacrifice while her father was all about sacrificing anyone who got in his way. They were diametrically opposed, standing stubbornly at the two poles, glaring at one another across a courtroom or a construction site or a meeting table, on and on forever. Would it ever end?

Probably not. At least not until one of them died.

Her friends—if they still considered themselves to be—exchanged confused looks. At that moment, they probably thought asking her for help had been a mistake, that she was a double agent or something. Understandable. Their little mountain community seemed really tight-knit with lots of familial ties. They couldn't possibly understand how Persia could turn her back on her father and become his foe. She'd loved him once upon a time, but he'd left too much destruction in his wake for her to ever respect him again. And not just environmentally.

Persia didn't need to look around the table to know they were questioning where her loyalties lay. Even as she stared down her own father, their shocked gazes burned her flesh with their suspicions she was a traitor. Or a plant. Some kind of sleeper cell, just waiting to pounce on unsuspecting victims. Like father, like daughter. The apple doesn't fall far from the tree. A chip off the old block.

Nothing could be further from the truth, but she couldn't tell them that. Not at that moment. Not with *him* smirking down at her, as if she were giving some childhood performance no one liked but had to suffer through to boost the kid's confidence.

Maybe she should have bailed on the meeting as she'd been so tempted to do. Not because facing Dick McNish scared her—it didn't. What *really* scared her was the thought Warren might believe his initial assumption. After researching his proposal, she'd realized how brilliant it really was. It deserved to be presented, not just for the sake of Wolf Woods, but he'd earned the right. Naturally, she fully expected her father to be pissy about it, but maybe the new offer and the evidence regarding the stink beetle might make him do the right thing for once, as unlikely as that might seem.

Dick finally sat at the head of the table and waited. With all eyes trained intently on her, Persia cleared her throat and shuffled the files and paperwork in front of her. She wasn't there to play around. It wasn't a family counseling session. She was there to do her damn job. And by god she was going to do it. So, she heaved a deep breath and slid directly into lawyer mode.

"Thank you for taking this meeting with us, Da—" she coughed to cover up her faux pas "—Mr. McNish. We come from opposing sides of the issue, the issue being the future and preservation of local lands, which carry an immense amount of historical, cultural, and environmental value. Not only is the land in question integral to the survival and livelihoods of the local community, but the woods are also home to another creature worthy of preserving: the blue marmorated stink beetle, which is a protected species found only in these woods."

"The...*what*?" McNish repeated with a little chortle as he leaned back in his chair. "We're here to talk about a *beetle?* Really?"

Persia's jaw clenched involuntarily as she turned her withering gaze in her father's direction. "Yes. But it's not just us who are worried about protecting this threatened species. I'm sure I don't need to educate you on how our government tends to react regarding the preservation and protection of such species. The courts will almost always side in favor of defending nature, particularly when an endemic species is at risk."

"Almost always," he retorted. "Those are your operative words, princess."

"I'm not your princess," she shot back, letting her resentment toward her father get the better of her.

Not anymore.

"Hmm, not anymore, it seems." He echoed her thought. He folded his arms over his chest and glanced around at everyone with mild amusement. "Is that the best you could come up with? I can't build homes that would bring in jobs and stimulate the local economy because of a *bug?*"

"Actually, we assumed you wouldn't be moved by the plight of an endangered species and suddenly halt all construction." Warren's voice spilled from his lips like molasses on a hot day. At least that's the effect it had on her nervous system, soothing her and heating her up at the same time.

"That so?" McNish tilted his head, ignoring Warren and giving her a curious look.

"That's right," she continued, flipping through the folder in front of her. "Mr. Edgecomb here came up with an alternate plan for your development—a plan that would benefit both sides equally."

She slid a stack of photos and paperwork across the table to her father and waited while he scanned them. His brow furrowed, and then his eyes grew wide for a moment before he caught himself.

"What the hell is this, Persia?" he demanded.

"It's an opportunity. That's what it is. The property is on the site of an abandoned chicken farm on the other side of town and it's been on the market for years."

Dick looked less than impressed. "That's your big proposal? A smelly, old chicken farm?"

Persia leaned toward her father, no long worrying about keeping up appearances. She had to convince him Warren's proposal was the best solution for everyone.

"Daddy, listen to me. The city seized the property a few years ago for unpaid taxes. I called them and you could get the land for a tiny fraction of what Wolf Woods will cost. For more land! That *has* to appeal to you."

Dick didn't react, just continued leafing through the papers and photos. That was his favorite stalling strategy, but Persia didn't want to give him time to think of a way to refuse. If she kept pushing the pros of Warren's plan, maybe…

"You always talk a big game about building up local communities and economies. This is the perfect chance to do that. Snatch up that land for a song and turn it from an eyesore into something people want to see. Wolf Woods remain wild for tourists and locals, as well as the beetle. Everyone wins. Just look at those photos, Daddy. I know you can see the potential."

She knew her father better than anyone in the room, yet even Persia couldn't read his face. The concept was sound, but he had a stubborn streak she'd inherited.

"I'd think by now you'd want a little positive PR, Mr. McNish." Warren's warning drew her attention for a moment.

She loved his passion, but her father wouldn't appreciate being reminded of the bad press he'd been dealing with lately. Strangely, though, he didn't seem bothered.

"That's old news, son. People have a short attention span these days. Tomorrow some random celebrity will get pulled over for drunk driving and I'll be forgotten."

"You sure about that?" Zeke sneered.

Persia warned him with a silent glance and Val laid a steadying hand on his arm. He needed to reel it back in. There was no use trying to start a fight. Her father would simply walk away if Zeke continued pressing. Then they'd be right back where they'd started.

"Imagine the goodwill and trust you'd earn within the community if you took over that chicken ranch and turned it into something beautiful," Persia continued. "A beloved landmark would remain for future generations, plus you'd save a ton of money on the land."

"Sure," her father admitted, "but it would require more work, which means hiring more people."

"Perfect," Val added. "More jobs for the locals equal even more goodwill."

“And on a more personal level,” Persia said, “you wouldn’t have to deal with my protest group anymore. I’m sure you would jump at the chance to remove that particular thorn from your side.”

“On top of that, you could start building right away,” added Warren.

McNish pursed his lips as he stared at a photo of the ranch, taking it all in with his fingers steepled in front of him. Persia couldn’t help holding her breath as she waited for his next move. For a brief moment, he looked to be actually considering Warren’s proposal. She should have known better.

Leaning back in his chair, he leveled a smug smile at his daughter and gave her a patronizing slow-clap. “Well done, princess. Well done. A for effort.”

Fury and humiliation blazed in her for thinking he might actually consider anything she brought to the table. “This isn’t a school project, Mr. McNish. I don’t want or need your approval. What I *do* want is an answer to this very serious proposal.”

“Mmm hmm. Of course. Yes. Very serious.”

No one could piss her off like her condescending, cruel dad. Closing the folder with a snap, he slid it across the table as if he couldn’t get it far enough away from him. He cast a complimentary nod at Warren.

"Good effort, but honestly, I like my original plan much better. Really, who wants to live on Gizzard Road or Chickenshit Lane? I know I wouldn't!"

She'd come into the meeting suspecting he'd blow her off on principle alone, but she still had one more card to play.

"I know something else you won't want, Mr. McNish. If you don't give up your plans for Wolf Woods and switch over to the chicken ranch, first thing tomorrow morning I'll file an injunction against McNish Development Corporation on behalf of the protected blue marmorated stink beetle. That will be a *federal* judge, Daddy. Not some county or state schlub you can bribe with your dirty money."

A vein deep in her father's neck pulsed quickly, barely noticeable on the surface, but she recognized it as his tell. She had him on the ropes. But as soon as it appeared, it disappeared, replaced by his more typical smirk as he stood. Reaching over, he patted Persia on the head like she was some kind of well-behaved puppy.

"That's right, princess. Put that law degree I paid for to work."

CHAPTER NINE

WARREN FELT AN OVERPOWERING URGE TO LEAP ON DICK McNish's back and tear him to shreds as they watched him saunter out of the trailer. Murdering his mate's father probably wasn't the best way to convince Persia they're fated to be together. Besides, the smell of his pack mates' anger at Persia drew his attention away from the slimeball walking out.

One by one and without a word, they filed out of the trailer, unable to tolerate remaining in the close confines of a trailer filled with McNish's nasty scent. They were just in time to watch the asshole peel out of the parking lot in his late-model BMW, throwing them a cocky waggle of his fingers out the window.

As soon as he sped out of sight, Val spun on her. "What the ever-loving *fuck?*"

"I know," Persia grimaced, as if expecting their wrath and willing to take it.

"What happened to Moonshadow, Ms. *McNish*?" Zeke growled.

"That's just my protestor name," she tried to explain, clearly eager for them to believe her. "No one uses their real names."

Warren wanted to believe her, but how could he? His wolf insisted she'd never been dishonest, but his human half didn't agree. It wasn't as if she'd fibbed about her weight or how fast she could type. This was a major omission, one that shook his very faith in her.

"Fine, but you still should have told us he was your dad," Val insisted. "Why did you lie?"

"She's a lawyer, remember?" Zeke snapped, as if that explained everything. Val sniffed in disgust masked as amusement.

"We need to give her a chance to explain herself." Warren surprised everyone, including himself. He wasn't defending her exactly. Not yet, anyway. Turning a hard look on her, he demanded, "So explain."

Persia sighed. "I use Moonshadow to fit in with the other protestors and to…" She chewed on her cheek for a second, as if debating whether to admit everything. "And to keep them from knowing he's my dad. If they did…"

"They wouldn't trust you?" Zeke finished, arching an ironic eyebrow at her.

Persia's fair skin flamed pink as she struggled to find the words necessary to incite trust from the rest of them. She was backed into a corner, and he hated it. Fate had brought them together, in an odd way perhaps, but the deed was done. Persia was his fated mate, and nothing and no one would ever be able to convince him otherwise. But his primary duty was to protect the pack, no matter what. Yet here stood his mate, the daughter of their most dangerous enemy.

He should have realized the truth. Wolves were known for their sniffers, and he should have caught the familial scent between Persia and Dick. Maybe it was the patchouli that clung to her like a skunk's stench. Maybe it was the fact matcha and nag champa covered the connection better than perfume. Maybe it was denial on his part. He didn't know for sure, but he couldn't ignore the feelings of betrayal eating at him.

The truth of the matter was that Warren knew more about Persia than Zeke and Val—and probably even McNish. Their one-way conversations when he was in his wolf form had proven she truly wanted to stop her father. Of course, Zeke would argue that she could easily have been aware of the pack's true nature and had been feeding Daddy Dearest every bit of information she could.

“How do we know you aren’t a plant, that you’re not feeding your dad everything you can about us?” Zeke snarled.

Warren felt a headache coming on. “Zeke, she’s not—” he started, but Persia interrupted him, her eyes sparkling with unshed tears.

“You have to believe me—”

“That’s where you’re wrong,” Zeke cut her off.

“Hey, guys!”

They all froze mid-sentence, slowly turning at the sound of heavy boots pounding on asphalt. Randy Leeper hurried toward them, holding something in his arms. Probably another bouquet of wildflowers. He stumbled to a stop in front of them and held out his hands, grinning proudly.

“Mew?” A tiny grey kitten poked its head over Randy’s fingers and chewed on his thumb adorably.

Val and Zeke stared at the kitten like they’d never seen a cat before. Certainly, they’d never seen a murderous asshole-turned-toddler cooing over one, anyway.

“Where did you find—” Val started and then stopped when a diesel engine fired up behind them and the smell of popcorn filled the air.

Even though they hadn't mated yet, Warren felt Persia's distress over the situation. It was no wonder she'd slipped away as soon as Randy had distracted them. By the time they all turned toward where she'd parked, her Westfalia was rolling out of the parking lot, leaving the smell of a movie theatre lobby in her wake.

"Of course she'd use biodiesel," Zeke snorted.

"Well, shit," Val said. "Are we chasing her, or what?"

"No point," Zeke replied, heading for their SUV with clenched fists.

Doors slammed and soon they were on their way back to the pack house, Zeke's anger overpowering them all. It wasn't as if Warren had been pleased to learn the news of Persia's parentage, but Zeke and Val's reaction had been unwarranted, considering all the help Persia had offered.

"You know, we might have learned more about her and her father if you two hadn't jumped down her throat like that," he pushed the words through clenched teeth.

"Excuse me?" Zeke shot him a bone-chilling look in the rearview mirror.

Bucking tradition, Warren scowled right back at his alpha. He wasn't about to back down where his mate was concerned. No, he didn't like the fact she'd hidden a vital piece of information from them, but facts were facts.

Persia was his mate and he sensed she hadn't been playing a double agent.

"You two acted like she was McNish himself."

"That's because she *is* a McNish, knucklehead," Zeke growled, returning his blazing gaze back to the road. "Whatever she's done so far, she's still his daughter. That's a bond that goes soul deep, Warren. We can't trust her anymore. Hell, I don't know if I can even trust you since you think she's your mate."

Warren's loyalty had never been called into question. Ever. And he wasn't about to allow it now.

"How can you say that to me, Zeke? Of all people. After all we've been through?"

Zeke's shoulders slumped and he sighed. "Fine. I do trust you for the most part, but come on, man. You thought Chloe was your mate for years. Look how that turned out."

"I was wrong then. I'm not wrong now."

"Sure…" Zeke grumbled.

Warren's teeth felt like they might be ground to nubs by how tightly he clenched his jaw. "I understand your hesitation, but I don't think Persia is my mate, Zeke. I *know*, and I'd appreciate a little support. Just like how I supported you when you decided a random human was *your* mate."

Frankly, it wouldn't have surprised Warren in the slightest if Zeke had pulled over so they could settle their beef on the side of the road. But instead Val stifled an amused smirk at all the testosterone zipping through the SUV and Zeke shot him a warning glance in the mirror.

"You've been a good and faithful beta, Warren, so I'm going to let that one slide. Don't push it."

Warren knew when to shut his mouth. Pack politics were about more than just pecking order. For a pack to survive, all members had to work within a very specific hierarchy. Sassing the alpha—even when you were his second-in-command—could get your ass handed to you. If any other pack members had been with them, Warren would have faced sharper blowback for his jibe. It was a testament to Zeke's respect for his beta that he gave him some latitude.

"Regardless of what you think about her, Warren, I'm in charge of protecting the pack, and I'm not about to get blindsided by McNish again. Until I have proof I can trust her, she might as well be McNish himself."

That didn't sound promising. "Any ideas on what might earn your trust?"

"Only when she pledges her loyalty to the pack will I fully trust her. But first, since you're so damned sure this one is your mate, you'll have to give her the claiming bite and transform her into one of us. Do that, and we can talk about our trust issues again."

"B-but..." his head swiveled between Zeke and Val. "She doesn't even know what we are."

Zeke shrugged. "Not my problem. If you want me to trust her, the ball's in your court."

Warren slumped back into his seat and stared out the window as the scenery blew by in a blur. When Zeke had discovered Val was his fated mate, he'd had a leg up Warren didn't have. Val had known about werewolves for years by the time they'd met. Persia was as clueless as most other humans. Werewolves were the stuff of movies and folklore, not reality hidden in plain sight.

How would a woman react to not only learning the truth, but then also being told she was destined to be the mate of such a mythical creature? Not well, he figured. He'd have to move slowly, but fast enough that Zeke would trust her before it was too late. It would be a delicate balance.

The SUV sped past the entrance to Wolf Woods along the forested highway. Persia's van sat parked near the campsite and his heart lurched just a little that she hadn't returned to Trina's cabin. Looking inward for guidance, he thought for a moment and then nodded.

He knew what he had to do.

CHAPTER TEN

What a fucking shitty day. First, she'd woken up in a strange place with a headache that could fell an elephant, and then it had just gone downhill from there. For a minute there, she'd thought things had started looking up. Then her new local friends—her *only* friends, she realized as she glanced around the circle of hippies holding hands as they laid their grievances at her feet—had turned on her. No doubt they had every reason to distrust her, but she'd hoped her work to save the woods they loved would give her some footing.

Apparently not.

Getting yelled at by people she actually *liked* had been bad enough, but then the shit had really hit the fan when she pulled into camp.

"I called this circle because we need to hash some things out," Leaf announced, apparently the leader of this little "peace circle."

Every single protestor held hands in a circle in the woods, staring at her as if she'd killed a puppy or something.

"Come on, you guys," she started, but Leaf held up a wooden spoon.

"It's not your turn to hold the truth stick, Moonshadow. Or should I say, Miss McNish."

Good lord, would this day never end? "How many times do I have to tell you? It's *Persia*."

As Leaf blathered on about how Persia had hurt his precious fee-fees—leaving out the fact he was a loser and a user—she did her best to contain her quickly spiraling emotions. Of course, any day in which she had to face her asshole of a father was automatically doomed. She'd long since given up hoping for any kind of meaningful interaction with him. He was just too cruel, too selfish, too…much. They'd never see eye-to-eye, which was something she would have been able to accept and move past if he wasn't so deliberately heartless.

Others might not understand but cutting him out of her life felt right. It hadn't been easy, and honestly had taken quite a long time, but she was comfortable with her decision at this point in her life. It wasn't her job to bring him around to the side of right, and it was a futile effort anyway. He had no soul to appeal to any longer. It had been replaced by piles and piles of wealth. He might have all the dollars to hire people to care for him in his old age, but they wouldn't *care* for him. Not like family. But that was the destiny he'd chosen for himself.

Leaf passed the "truth stick" to Summer, who stood next to him with perfectly shimmering tears in her big blue eyes. "My truth is that I'm feeling very vulnerable. And under attack. By you, Persia. By you and your lies," she sniffled.

"Oh, good god," Persia muttered, dropping Leaf's hand to pinch the bridge of her nose.

"Thank you for sharing your truth, Summer," Leaf declared, shooting a righteous glare at Persia and grabbing her hand back roughly.

Summer dabbed at her eyes pitifully and passed the spoon on to Toby, who started in on a seemingly endless rant about honor and trust and something about the goddess moon.

None of this nonsense mattered, not compared to the way her friends had looked at her. One in particular. He hadn't accused her of betrayal like Zeke and Val, but the confusion and pain in his sad blue eyes had nearly torn her in two. That right there was why she no longer used her legal name, except when necessary. The questions, the stares, the silent accusations were too much to take. She'd thought about changing it legally, but the idea of signing court documents as Persia Moonshadow was almost as unthinkable.

Who knew how it had happened? Word of her heritage had spread like wildfire, and before she'd even made it back to camp, all the protestors had heard the news and demanded she join a peace circle. The hits just kept on coming.

"I just think it's, like, really gross that you've been pretending to care about the environment when really you're totally just trying to get your dad's attention or whatever," Rustle sniped, pulling Persia from her reverie.

"Seriously, Rustle? You really think I'm doing this for *him*? Dick McNish doesn't have a bigger enemy than me."

"Again, Moonshadow, you have to wait your turn to hold the truth stick," Leaf interjected.

"Persia!" she screamed at the top of her lungs, making everyone jump a little.

Taking a deep breath, she concentrated on holding back her rage at these assholes for questioning her ethics. Lower level college psych professors would have told her that her anger was simply projection, but she hadn't listened to them then, and she wasn't about to start now. Eventually, the person next to her finished their little speech—which was the same as all the others—and passed the "truth stick" to her.

"My turn, huh?" She glowered at every single idiot standing in that fucking circle. "First of all, let me remind you all that if it weren't for me, none of you would be here right now. *I'm* the one who organized this ragtag little group of high-school dropouts and bored trust-fund kids. *I'm* the one who encouraged you all to give a shit about more than just smoking weed and playing with your didgeridoos and your hacky sacks. *I'm* the one who taught you all what is at stake if we don't fight to protect our planet. *I'm* the one who showed you how to turn your lack of ambition into something meaningful. *I'm* the one who brought you all together, who keeps this operation up and running."

"Now, wait just a minute—" Leaf tried to interject, but Persia shook the wooden spoon in his face. "Uh, uh, uh, I have the truth stick now, and I'm speaking my fucking truth." Leaf pressed his lips into a thin, hard line and, to his credit, shut the hell up. "I will *never* give up fighting for this planet. No matter who I have to go up against. And yes, that includes my father. I have done more than enough to prove to all of you that I'm on the right side, that I'm doing good things for this world. And if you don't like the fact I just so happen to be related to that sociopath, then quite frankly, you can all go fuck your hippie-dippie-selves!"

She held the spoon out from her body and mic-dropped it, although the effect was less than satisfying. Leaf stepped aside as she stormed out of the circle, biting the inside of her cheek to keep herself from crying. Every cell in her body boiled with rage. Mostly at herself.

The protestors back at camp hadn't deserved to be the brunt of her anger. Yes, their new age ways sometimes got on her nerves, but they were kind, loving people who were at least *trying* to do the right thing. Some were smarter than others, and some were total morons. The problem was that they couldn't see past their own noses. They didn't realize the war she was waging wasn't just about Wolf Woods. It was about stopping her father's reign of terror. But their hearts were generally in the right place.

However, hers seemed to have gone astray.

Her thoughts turned to Warren, all sweaty and bulging as he maneuvered a slab of plywood into position halfway up a giant tree. No fear, no hesitation, just action. And hotness. All the hotness!

Branches whipped across her cheek and thorny shrubs pulled at the flesh of her calves as she hiked deeper into the woods, heading for the one place where she would feel safe again—the clearing. The pain was a welcome distraction from the deep ache she felt for Warren.

The sun still dappled the clearing as she stumbled into it, finding her favorite animal in the world sitting in a circle of light. His tail thumped at her approach, and the tension in her body lightened and floated away on the gentle breeze.

"Hey, handsome." She knelt on the soft earth and petted his huge head.

He nuzzled her hand and then lay down on his side, drawing a chuckle from Persia. "Okay, hint taken."

She lay down perpendicular to the wolf and rested her head on his ribcage, a sense of calm flowing through her body with every gentle breath he took. The sky overhead reminded her of Warren's eyes, a perfect shade of blue. She sighed heavily and grabbed one of the wolf's forepaws in her hand. She held it gently, her thumb digging in between the pads and massaging the space between. The wolf groaned his pleasure.

"You would *not* believe the day I've had since lunch. Remember that couple who came here earlier and asked me to join their meeting with Dick McNish? Well, I may have omitted that he's my dad."

The wolf sniffed loudly, as if the name of her father affected him. "I know. I know. I'm an idiot. I should have told them beforehand. Then maybe they wouldn't have accused me of being a traitor. We want the same thing and I just love how down to earth they are, compared to the rest of my merry band of lunatics. Now they don't trust me, and I can't blame them. The worst part though—and I couldn't admit this to anyone else but you, my sweet friend—the worst part was seeing the betrayal in Warren's eyes. I don't know why. I mean, I barely know the guy, but…I really hate the idea of disappointing him."

She turned to look at the wolf, as if he really understood what she was saying. "Warren's the hottie local who's helping me with my platform. Would you believe I thought he was just eye candy? Nope. He's got brains too. He worked up a brilliant plan I thought for sure my dad would go for. Saved him money, bought goodwill with the locals, and would be an easier route for him overall. But did he have the good sense to see the benefits? Not my dad. Too stubborn. Guess the apple didn't fall too far from the tree after all."

Looking back at the sky, she snorted her amusement. "Of course, I hauled ass out of there as soon as they all accused me of backstabbing them. Then I got back to the camp to find everyone *there* mad at me. I have no idea how word spread so fast, but they all think I betrayed them too. In fact, that idiot Leaf called a peace circle to hash out all of our feelings."

The wolf lifted his head and gave her a curious look.

"It pretty much went down how you'd expect. Everyone took turns, venting about what an awful, horrible, lying sack of shit I am. But I got my turn at the end." Her cheeks pinked up over what she'd said. "Unfortunately, I was kind of a jerk to them. They're not all bad. Most have noble intentions and didn't deserve me ripping into them like that. I should have been more patient, but after the day I've had...I just didn't have the bandwidth to deal. So, I came out here to see you."

The wolf started panting, offering her his other paw for a mini massage.

"I dunno, maybe this is all a waste of time. Maybe I should find some other cause to fight for. I have no doubt everyone in my group would gladly pack up and get the hell out of Dodge first thing in the morning—maybe before I even get back. That would serve me right for how I spoke to them. Honestly, losing them wouldn't hurt half as much as losing the folks from the Soren village. If they abandon me because of who screwed my mother, that's when I'll know I've failed."

The wolf whined and reached over to lick her cheek.

"I know. It's depressing as hell. But judging by how pissed off their mayor was, I don't see how they'll ever trust me again. So, I ask you again, why bother? Might as well just pack up and head on down the road to lick my wounds."

At that, the wolf pulled himself out from under her, causing her head to drop to the grass. As she leaned up on her elbows, he sat a short distance away, staring at her intensely. Almost like he was trying to tell her something. When she moved closer to him, he took two steps back and sat again, that same almost-disappointed look on his face.

"Hey, was it something I said?" She tried to scoot closer again, but again he shimmied away, always leveling that hard look on her.

She squirmed under his scrutiny until it became uncomfortable. If he'd been human, she might have thought he was judging her for thinking of walking away from the fight with her father. Obviously her subconscious was working overtime.

"Hey, after the past twenty-four hours, I've earned the right to feel discouraged," she whined defensively.

The wolf remained motionless, his gaze burning her with shame.

"Fine, you're right, okay? I know that. Duh! I'm not going to give up just because I've had a bad day full of drama. If those protestors leave in the morning, fuck 'em. And fuck the Sorens too. Fuck anyone who doesn't think I can stop my father from spreading his evil greed across these beautiful, pristine woods."

Determination buzzed through her, energizing her with newfound resolve. She didn't need anyone's help. And maybe if Warren—er, the entire Soren village—maybe if they saw how hard she was working to thwart her dad, they might start to trust her again. Sitting upright, she grinned at her wolfy friend.

"They can question my motivations all they want. I'm still going to do everything in my power to stop him, to keep these woods wild. First things first, though. I need to get back and finish my platform. Then I'll go file that injunction first thing tomorrow. After that, it's just a waiting game, so I suppose I'll lie around on my... treehouse."

An image of Warren pounding nails into the platform popped into her head unbidden. His smile, his toned but not bulging biceps, his gentle and generous nature. She'd never met anyone quite like him. Maybe one day he could forgive her. If not, she'd survive, but life might be just that much duller.

Pulling herself to her feet, Persia planted her hands on her hips, a la Wonder Woman, and grinned down at the wolf. "Mark my words, friend. I won't come down out of that tree until I hear Wolf Woods will remain wild."

He barked his approval and then trotted off in the opposite direction from camp, as if that was what he'd been waiting to hear all along.

CHAPTER ELEVEN

WARREN SAT ON THE TREEHOUSE PLATFORM, THE LAST RAYS of the orange sunset warming the muscles of his bare chest and arms as he affixed a low railing. The little treehouse was shaping up to look like a proper, serviceable stand with enough room for a couple of people to lie down comfortably. He wiped the sweat from his brow and stared down at the camp, finding a familiar redheaded figure trudging across the clearing toward his tree.

Right on time.

Nobody would ever know, but Warren had probably set a record for how fast a wolf could run clear across the woods back to the camp via a roundabout loop. He'd jumped into his work pants as he headed for Persia's chosen tree but didn't bother with his shirt. Once he'd learned she liked the way he looked without it, he wondered if he could go his whole life shirtless just to impress her. Probably not, but building her treehouse was a perfect excuse.

None of the other protestors had tried to stop him from getting back to work, but they'd all been far too busy discussing the latest gossip about Persia to bother joining him. He'd barely caught his breath before he heard her progress through the woods. Quickly moving the rudimentary railing into place, he started nailing like mad until she came into view.

Stopping at the base of the tree, she looked up with wide-eyed surprise. "Warren?"

Her voice sounded like a whisper of hope on a cold, dark night. It broke his heart.

"Hey, what took you so long, Red? Figured I'd have a condo up here by the time you decided to help out."

A sea bass couldn't have done a better impression of a fish out of water, mouth opening and closing with nothing coming out except a few little squeaks. With a confused shake of her head, she tied a loose rope to the handle of her small toolbox and pulled on the other end of the rope.

"I'm coming up!" she called after he grabbed the toolbox. She ignored the suspicious, angry and hurt looks from the others as she climbed into her harness, which he'd deliberately left on the ground for her.

When she reached the tree limb, he extended a hand to hoist her onto the platform with him. Her eyes locked onto his broad, glistening torso and he pretended not to notice. He couldn't stop a smile from playing at his lips, though, so he quickly turned back to the railing before she caught him.

"I didn't want to broadcast this conversation by shouting up at you, but what are you doing here? Don't get me wrong. I'm glad, but after what happened earlier, I didn't think anyone from your village would be interested in helping me anymore."

He shrugged as he hammered a nail into the railing. "Have to admit I'm not a fan of being lied to." When she opened to her mouth to protest, he held up a hand to stop her. "Yeah, yeah, you didn't lie. I'll rephrase, counselor. I don't appreciate you keeping such a big secret from me… *us*."

Because mates don't keep secrets, he thought, but managed to swallow the words. They had a lot of ground to cover before they could be so open with each other. They'd get there, he knew it in his soul, he just needed to remain patient.

"I like to think I'm a good judge of character," he continued, glancing over his shoulder and catching her gaze skimming his back. Her fair skin stood no chance of hiding her embarrassment. "I'm certain you had your reasons for hiding your connection to McNish, but some people in my pa—" He covered the near-slip with a fake sneeze and continued. "Some people in my village don't exactly see it that way. They wonder how dedicated you are to your cause."

Pink turned to red in her cheeks, mottling along her neck and down her chest, where it disappeared under her shirt. The sadness in her eyes as they dropped to inspect the toes of her boots wrenched his gut.

"Not me," he quickly added, "or I wouldn't be here right now. But you have to understand that my people have been burned by strangers too often. That's hard for us to shake, Red."

Instead of arguing, she looked thoughtful for a moment and then met his eyes without a shred of defensiveness. "Your chicken farm plan is solid. That was some quick thinking that my father should have jumped at. Anyone else in the same position would have. Then again, maybe if anyone else but me had presented it, he would have."

Warren rolled back onto his ass, taking a much-needed break from being all sweaty and manly for her. "Maybe he'll see the light."

"Maybe." Though her tone held zero hope of that happening. "But that's not really his style. Railroading people *is* though. I think that's what really revs his engines, forcing people into positions where they have no other choice. And maybe I inherited that gene because I've already got all the paperwork ready to file first thing in the morning. It'll take time for the injunction to be granted, but I have no doubt it will. In the meantime..."

Warren grinned and patted the platform. "Home sweet home."

Persia grinned back, those dimples going all the way to China. "Exactly."

For the first time, she glanced around the platform, her gaze zeroing in on a pile of goods he'd dragged up the tree. A dark red eyebrow shot up and her blue-and-brown gaze turned on him with a questioning look.

"What?" He feigned innocence.

"What's that?"

"Hmm?" He glanced over his shoulder, as if he didn't know full well what she was talking about. "Just some food and a couple of sleeping bags."

"And why are there two?"

"One for each of us." He shrugged one shoulder and went back to nailing down the railing. "There. Low enough we won't roll off in the middle of the night. It's also big enough to sleep two comfortably."

"Whoa whoa whoa, slow your roll, Paul Bunyan." She shook her head. "What makes you think I'm letting you sleep on the same platform as me?"

He didn't really care if it pissed her off. No mate of his would sleep in a tree *alone* surrounded by randy hippies. Not gonna happen. "I told you I'd help you build a treehouse, Red. I never said anything about letting you sleep in one on your own."

"Excuse me? Who are you to *let* me do anything?"

"Listen, I don't really get the point of all this anyway, but if you're determined to sleep in a wall-less tree fort, the least I can do is give you a camping buddy. Me!"

A battle raged inside her, that much he could tell. Her pretty pink lips worked as if she was trying to form words, but the scent coming off her betrayed her arousal.

"You think I can't take care of myself?" she sniped, narrowing her gaze at him.

"I don't recall ever saying that."

"You thought it."

"Conjecture, counselor." He flashed her a sly smile.

She huffed her frustration. "Point is, I don't need anyone babysitting me."

"Who said anything about babysitting? I'm just here as your muscle, which you haven't seemed to mind so far, from what I can tell."

The color in her cheeks flamed, and Warren sensed a shift in her scent that told him he might not have crossed a line, but he had at least toed it.

"What the hell is that supposed to—"

Her volume had grown to the point Warren almost missed a sound that seemed out of place. Scooting close to her, he covered her mouth with his big palm. Obviously, she thought he was trying to stop her arguing, judging by the fire in her eyes, but one cautious finger to his lips stilled her. Then he pointed to the ground, where the sound of someone or something barreling through the trees echoed through the woods.

Then came the shouts and more leaves rustling until a few of the protestors ran toward their chosen trees. Several sheriff deputies chased after them, pulling them away from their half-finished projects before they could get a couple feet off the ground.

"You're under arrest for trespassing, you tree-hugging asshole!" a younger deputy shouted a little too eagerly as he pushed Leaf's face into the forest floor.

Warren released a stunned Persia as the scene repeated itself a few more times, until the deputies escorted the last of the protestors from the woods. More shouting and arguing rippled through the air from the direction of the campsite, which could only mean one thing. Every last protestor was being evicted. Not just evicted but arrested.

The effort was far too coordinated and far too violent for Warren's taste. It reeked of McNish's doing. The proud members of the Tremble PD were as honest as the day was long, which explained why the county cops had swooped in. McNish had probably greased the county Sheriff's palm to get the job done.

Warren and Persia had dropped low and lain on their stomachs, peering over the edge of their treehouse during the commotion. They remained silent and motionless as they watched the raid, instinctively knowing they were far more valuable to the cause if they remained in the tree than if they came down and allowed themselves to be arrested. That would serve no one but McNish.

The sound of the last Sheriff's cruiser driving off grew faint, and then silence overtook the woods at the same point the darkness of night engulfed them. Warren was about to say something when Persia shook her head. They waited a full five minutes before she finally sat up and rested her back against the tree trunk.

"Well, shit," she breathed, looking stunned, as far as he could tell in the dim light. "I can't believe my father did that. You know he was responsible for this. R-right?"

"I figured," Warren replied, leaning back next to her.

"I also can't believe none of them ratted us out. They knew we were up here, but they didn't say anything. Even after all the terrible things I said to them."

"Maybe those circle-jerkers like you more than you realize." He absently pulled out their sleeping bags.

She stared at him with a confused expression when he handed over hers. "H-how did you know about..." she started.

Oh shit. She'd spilled her guts to his *wolf* not *him*. A good offense was always the best defense, he decided.

"You're not as hard to read as you think, Red."

She seemed to buy it. "Guess not. Not a great trait for a lawyer, huh? Should we go bail them out?"

"Only if you're sure the Sheriff has the slightest inkling to set them free before all of this blows over in your dad's favor, which I can guarantee he doesn't." He was grim as he rolled out his sleeping bag.

She watched him with incredulity for a moment before responding. "You've got to be kidding me with that."

He grinned as he sat on the relative cushiness of the sleeping bag and pulled a bag of potato chips from the food stores he'd brought up. "Here's the way I see it, Red. You're not going to give up your advantage of leaving this tree. I'm not leaving you up here alone. Which means we're gonna be here for a while. Might as well get comfy."

CHAPTER TWELVE

Persia's legs dangled off the edge of the platform as she watched the embers of a few dying campfires flicker into oblivion. Just like her protest. A few minutes either way, and she would have found herself in the back of a squad car, just like Leaf and Summer and all the rest. Her father would be pissed she hadn't been tossed behind bars for the night, or longer, if he could somehow have managed it. Nothing made him happier than teaching her a lesson.

"How bad are the local cops?" She glanced back at Warren, who'd managed to find his shirt, much to her bitter disappointment.

Warren's big hand dragged through his mop of sandy hair, slicking back the part that was still damp from his sweat. When it was dry, his hair seemed pretty straight, only curling at the nape of his neck and temples when he'd been working hard. Darkness had fallen so heavily in the canopy of the woods she couldn't make out those kinds of details very well, and suddenly she wished for a lantern.

Spinning around, she focused on the silhouette of a nearby tree, trying to *not* think about the way her body reacted every time he came into view. Hell, every time she even thought about him. No stranger to animal attraction, Persia had never been so irresistibly drawn to anyone before. It was almost as if he was a bonfire and she was a hapless moth. With a firm head shake, she reminded herself—just as she had many times over the last day—she was there to do a job, not a local boy.

"The town cops are good guys," he finally answered, "but those county jerks..."

"So, they're evil?"

Warren snorted. "I'd say 'evil adjacent.' From what I've heard, your dad's had the sheriff and some of his deputies in his pocket for a while now."

"That sounds right," Persia sighed. "My dad has always used money to grease the wheels of what he calls progress. No matter where he goes, he manages to sniff out the people in charge who are most susceptible to taking bribes and breaking their oaths. It's like his superpower."

"Dirtbag," Warren sneered, then quickly added, "No offense."

Persia shook her mane of red hair. "You're joking, right? He's been a cold shadow looming over me since the day I was born. I think 'dirtbag' is too good for him."

Anger was herbal tea compared to the fury that pulsed through her veins at this latest salvo by good old Daddy Dearest. He'd gone too far this time. Eh, who was she kidding? He'd gone too far *many* times, but this was the last straw. Jumping to her feet, she grabbed her harness and strapped in.

"Hey, what the hell do you think you're doing?" Warren's voice was full of alarm.

Persia clipped the carabiner to her harness and gave it a good tug. "Duh, I'm going to bail them out. I can't just sit up here and twiddle my thumbs while they rot in some nasty backwater cells. No offense."

He didn't seem to hear the accidental insult as he scrambled to his feet and grabbed her belaying line. "Like hell!"

"I can't just sit here!" she fired back.

Warren let his eyelids fall shut as he took a deep breath, giving her the chance to take in the sharp line of his nose, the light stubble on his cheeks, the way his lips pressed together when she frustrated him. Damn, that would be heaven to see every day.

"Listen to me, Persia." He softened his tone and slipped his hand down to cover hers. It took all of her concentration to focus on his words after that. "We already talked about this. You can't risk getting arrested. If you go down there and some errant deputy is stationed out there somewhere, you'll join everyone else behind bars. Their sacrifice will mean nothing. You can't save Wolf Woods from a jail cell."

"I know, but it feels like I'm hiding up here instead of facing my dad head on."

Warren gently unclipped her from the harness and helped her out of it before she really knew what he was doing. All she knew was that his body was so close to hers, his knuckles skimming random spots on her body and causing her brain to spin around inside her skull like a top.

"If there's one thing I've learned, it's that you have to pick your battles wisely. Getting your pals out of jail may *seem* important, but they didn't rat you out for a reason. Even if they were angry with you, they knew you're the only person who has a snowball's chance in a Georgia summer of winning against your father."

She gingerly stepped out of the harness, one hand grasping Warren's taut bicep for leverage. Yeah…*leverage.* He dropped the harness to the platform and gripped her shoulders, turning her into a yearning pile of mush as she stared into his eyes—what she could see of them, anyway.

"Persia, we didn't build this spectacular treehouse just so you could sit in jail. If you get arrested, you have to know I'll come after you, even if that means I get arrested too. That would leave the forest vulnerable. No one would be left to defend it from the bulldozers your dad is itching to bring in here."

The urge to stand on her tiptoes and lay one on those luscious lips nearly overpowered her. Clearing the lust from her throat, she sidestepped him to put some much-needed space between them.

Then she smiled. "You keep surprising me, Warren."

There was plenty of light to see his sexy grin. "Good. Hope that never ends." Then he clapped his hands, dug around in his boxes of supplies and turned back to offer her a can. "Beer? After today, I know I need one."

"No," Persia glanced back to where the last bits of red glowed in the campers' fire pits. "Eh, screw it. Gimme."

She snatched the beer from his hand and sat on her sleeping bag, back against the tree. As the ice-cold IPA slid down her throat, she groaned with relief. A shot of tequila might have flooded her with warmth more quickly, but nothing beat a good beer at the end of a long day. Beer and chips weren't the only things Warren had hauled up to the platform, which she discovered when he passed her half a turkey sandwich.

"Wow, you really came prepared." She accepted the sandwich gratefully.

"What can I say? I'm a Boy Scout." He dug around again in his stores and whipped out a faded, tattered *Free Tibet!* flag.

"Is that my—"

He grinned. "Yup! Thought you might like a touch of home."

As they munched and drank their beers, another complication popped into Persia's head. "What am I going to do tomorrow? I need to file that injunction first thing. If I don't, we won't have a chance in hell of beating my father."

"Don't worry your pretty little head. It's not like this is the Ritz. Pretty sure you'll be awake at the crack of dawn. I'll call Zeke so someone can distract any deputies still on stake-out and I'll stay here. No problem. But you'll want to get your sweet ass back up this tree ASAP, just in case."

Persia took a long draught of the bitter ale and winced. Not at the taste, but at what still lay ahead of her. "I just can't stand the thought of that asshole winning again."

She felt Warren's eyes on her, studying her. "Mind my asking what's up with your relationship with him? I don't mean to be blunt, but it seems sorta fucked up."

Persia snorted at his observation. "Yeah, you could say that."

Where to start? She drained her beer and when she handed him the empty, it was instantly replaced with a fresh one. A few sips later, she finally had the nerve to continue.

"Honestly, it's not really all that complicated. Sitting here in this tree, I see my life as two parts. The first half was when I was young and naive. Happy. Convinced my father could do no wrong, that he truly meant all the bullshit he spouted about doing good. Throughout my childhood, he encouraged me to be ambitious, to put all my energy and focus into my future. Looking back, a solid work ethic is the one positive thing he taught me. Of course, he couldn't have known all my hard work would turn around to bite him in the ass."

"And your mom?"

Persia sighed and drained her second beer just so she could talk about her mother. "She's… around. Well, not really." She sighed again, giving him an amused grimace. "It's a whole deal. My dad's talent is working hard. My mom's is playing hard."

Warren waited patiently as she figured out the best way to explain her twisted family dynamic. No one on this planet she was trying to save could ever accuse her of having a hard life. She'd grown up white, straight and more privileged than most. So many people had it so much worse than she could ever imagine. But, as the saying went, everyone had shit to deal with.

"We were never close, my mom and me. She always maintained a solid distance from me, both literally and figuratively. While Daddy worked his ass off, Mother traveled. It's her passion. I think she only had me because Daddy expected offspring. After I was born, that was it for her. She took off on cruises, yoga retreats, European tours, you name it. For my sixteenth birthday, she flew me to Paris to go shopping and I hated every minute. If it's not obvious, *haute couture* wasn't made for my body type."

Warren's gaze traveled the length of her body, turning her insides to hot mush. "Looks pretty perfect to me," he mumbled, barely loudly enough for her to hear.

"Anyway." Her brain struggled to keep them on track while her body reminded her they were alone… in a forest… in a tree… with sleeping bags, chips and beer. "Mother likes luxury and Daddy… well, I guess he likes keeping her busy elsewhere."

"So, were you close to your father growing up?"

"More than with Mother, but it was almost like a business relationship. From my birth, I was always Daddy's Little Girl. He spoiled me some, I won't lie, but mostly he taught me to follow in his footsteps. I think he was hoping I'd become a mini version of him."

Warren choked on his beer and then chuckled, wiping his face dry. "Yeah, that didn't work out so well for him. Did it? You're nothing like him."

Her heart warmed at that. "Thanks for that, but even I know we have similarities. But I'll be honest, there was a time when my deepest desire was to be just like him. During Part One of my life. Part Two started when I learned the truth."

Warren sat up a bit. "About what?"

"About him. My father. About what his actual business model looks like. During my youth, he'd been involved with all of these environmental agencies. If you can believe it, he pushed me to go into environmental law. As far as I knew, he was an esteemed philanthropist, the kind of wealthy man who uses his money for good causes. I held him on such a pedestal, he could have touched the sun."

"What happened?"

"I'd just been hired as a junior associate at a well-respected environmental firm. My job was basically to stuff thousands of pages of documents into file folders in these massive shelves that moved with a push of a button. It was deathly boring, and the hours were grueling, but I loved it. I was on my way! One night, a bunch of us younger staff members went to happy hour at a nearby bar. When I broke off to hit the bathroom, this woman followed me and started chatting. Turns out she was a reporter, and I was completely unprepared for the bombshell she dropped on me. She told me, not so politely, about my father's strong-arming tactics, how he only pretends to be environmentally conscious to keep the tree huggers off his back, that basically he was the exact kind of guy I wanted to fight against. At first, I thought she was just trying to pick a fight or something, but she had documentation and eyewitness accounts to back up her claims."

"Damn, some happy hour that turned out to be."

Even during a hard talk, Warren somehow managed to lighten her mood. "After that, my world flipped upside down. It all became clear. My father wanted me to be an environmental lawyer to help *him*, not the planet. He'd used his influence to get me the job, so the first thing I did was quit. The people there seemed dedicated to saving the planet, but I couldn't allow my future to be tainted like that. Before he officially cut me off, I stopped taking his money. I used my last paycheck from the firm to buy Betty, and I've spent the last few years being a thorn in his side. And that's pretty much my tale of woe. Are you crying yet?"

He chuckled and took her empty can from her fingers. "I can definitely understand why you choose to use a different name."

"Once I started making noise about him, it became hard to win people's trust after they learned I'm the child of the monster we're all trying to stop."

Warren's thick, warm fingers found her empty hand and clasped it gently. "For what it's worth, I trust you. One thousand percent, no matter what anyone else thinks. You're a good person with a good heart."

That heart picked up its pace in her chest at his touch and kind words. Not to mention the gleam of adoration in his eyes—although that could have simply been the moon peeking through the canopy.

"Thank you," she whispered, barely able to choke out the words past the emotions consuming her. "That means... a lot."

She'd never had an ally like Warren, and it felt nice. It felt even nicer that *Warren* was her ally, not some random guy she'd met at a protest. Which, of course, he was. Yet... he wasn't. The confusing feelings needed to stop. She needed to focus, and not on herself. It was time to turn the tables and put the focus on him.

"Enough about me." She couldn't manage to pull her hand from his. It felt too nice. "What about you? What's your family like? Please tell me it's not as dysfunctional as mine."

"Not even close. Pretty normal, really. Parents who loved us, a great sister, a tight-knit community, and friends I can truly depend on. I'd risk my life for any one of them, and I know in my soul the feeling is mutual. I may just look like a poor, dumb redneck, but in my personal opinion, *I'm* the privileged one here."

Persia burst out laughing, sliding a few inches closer to him as her body shuddered. "I would have to agree with you there, Warren. I have no clue how that feels. The protesters I recruit come and go like the wind, so I don't even have what I would consider to be real friends. I wonder if I'll ever find a place that feels like home."

Silence drew out between them so long she glanced over to him. The darkness did nothing to hide the intensity in his gaze.

"Maybe you already have."

Her brain screamed for her to tell him to lay off the hard sell, but her mouth wouldn't obey. All it wanted to do was press against those lips she'd daydreamed of. In that moment, it truly hit her that she liked Warren. A lot. Too much, even. And the dream of finally belonging somewhere—and with *him* to boot—was too tempting to ignore. For all his mysterious ways and his quiet, country boy persona, Warren was starting to feel…safe. Whenever they were together, it felt as if that was exactly where every decision in her life had led her. Like she belonged. Like she was home.

CHAPTER THIRTEEN

A BLAST OF CRISP, AUTUMN AIR WOKE WARREN WITH A start. It was still dark out, too dark to see anything except the pale moonlight glittering through the canopy. Instincts had him sniffing the air, but nothing out of the ordinary caught his attention. Except one thing.

Persia.

Finally coming awake and fully into his human senses, he slowly turned his head to find Persia's back pressed up against his front, spooning him. Blinking a few times to make sure he wasn't imagining things, he was happily surprised to find himself staring at the back of her head, her red curls splayed over her shoulder and his left arm, the same one on which her head rested. His right arm twitched, wanting to pull her tighter, but he didn't want to wake her.

He wanted this moment to last forever.

The way her chest rose and fell under his arm, the faint smell of her shampoo under her more powerful and intoxicating personal scent, how her body fit so perfectly against his, despite the thick fabric of two sleeping bags between them. Dammit, he knew he should have zipped their bags together to make one giant sleeping bag!

Of course, she wouldn't have put up with that, not last night, when she'd already been irritated with him. Honestly, he was surprised she hadn't rolled him off the edge of the platform in his sleep. Good thing he'd built that railing.

Persia stirred, her ass pressing up against the spot that really didn't need to be any more alert than it already was, yet he silently begged for more. He could have remained like that for the rest of the night, his cock thrumming against the sleeping bag, but she hadn't finished moving in her sleep. Rolling around inside her bag, she snuggled up to his warmth, facing him, and then sighed peacefully.

In that moment, Warren knew joy. The simple joy of holding his mate, breathing her in, reveling in every inch of her without even touching her flesh. Whatever he might have felt about Chloe in the past was nothing compared to how he felt with Persia so close. Zeke and Val could scoff all they wanted, but he knew. He *knew*.

For no reason in particular—or maybe because somewhere deep in her unconscious, she felt their bond too—Persia's eyes fluttered open. Even in the dark, he could make out the difference between her blue eye and her brown eye, and both stared at him with such profound vulnerability, his breath stopped in his chest. She'd never looked so open, so trusting.

Unguarded Persia.

A stray red curl drifted onto her cheek and Warren felt it was his duty to brush it back into place with his finger. She didn't stop him. She didn't even stop staring up at him with that sweet expression, and he found the rest of his fingers cupping her cheek gently as his thumb brushed across her lips. Instead of pulling away or telling him to "slow his roll," Persia allowed her eyelids to fall shut and released a whisper of a sigh. That was all the invitation Warren needed.

Warren ran his fingers through her hair, far enough to fist the glorious strands. He tugged her head back to expose the long line of her neck and she drew in a sharp breath, mouth falling open with her gasp.

He lowered his head and caressed her with his lips, peppering her with kisses and savoring her breathy sigh. He licked and tasted her, taunting them both when he gently worried her skin between his teeth. That earned him a sharp squeak and his heart raced with her obvious enjoyment.

He cupped her breast with his free hand, her nipple stiff under the thin fabric that separated them. She stroked him, her palm sliding across his chest and fingers curling to drag her nails over his taut muscles. Desire consumed him, the knowledge that she wanted him driving his need even higher. He breathed deeply and savored the scent of her arousal, the sweet musk luring his beast to the surface —encouraging and tormenting him.

Right about then he was grateful they hadn't zipped their sleeping bags together—the fabric acting as a barrier to keep them apart. He still needed to tell her the truth about werewolves before he gave her the claiming bite. It was a plain and simple fact and now wasn't the time for that conversation. But that didn't mean he had to stop. As long as he didn't fuck her—claim her—he'd be fine. Right?

He brought his lips to hers, capturing her mouth as he sought to drive her mad with kisses. She inhaled and tensed with the first kiss but melted a moment later and arched into his touch. She pushed to get closer and he savored her nearness. Their shared passion increased, kisses going from slow and lazy to harsh and aggressive— his tongue invading her mouth and taking what he craved. She pressed against him and they practically fought for power, the meeting of their mouths and shared touches growing more and more aggressive.

Persia released him and reached down, sliding along his front as far as she could within his sleeping bag. They struggled with the thick fabric, finding themselves at an awkward angle neither of them were willing to abandon. She seemed to know what she was after and she was going to get it. Her fingers brushed Warren's thick shaft and then quickly wrapped around his length.

He stiffened further at her touch, the feel of her squeezing him. She explored his dick, from thick base to the bulging tip and back again. He felt as if his body showed off for her, thicker and warmer than usual, responding to her with more sensitivity.

Warren returned the favor without hesitation. He stretched his arm down into her bag, surrounded by her warmth until he reached her thighs. He stroked her and she changed position, opening her legs to give him a better angle—more space. He brushed her pussy and warm breath fanned his face when she released a delighted sigh. But it wasn't enough. Not nearly. And he wasn't about to let the sleeping bag remain in his way. Even if that meant losing her touch.

He scooted forward and urged Persia to turn, firm yet gentle dominance that she submitted to without hesitation. She wasn't a pushover by any stretch of the imagination. Knowing that he had earned her trust to let him move her suffused him with pride.

With one hand he cupped her breast and squeezed, brushing a thumb over the hard point of her nipple. She shivered with his touch and he transferred his gentle grip to her other breast, doing the same thing. He grinded his cock against her ass, spooning her with his heated body and rubbing his need against the mounds of her ass. He listened to every soft, breathy moan and groan, the sounds coming more frequently the longer he teased her. When the scent of her arousal nearly tossed him past the edge of his control, he gave himself permission to reach down.

He dipped his fingers beneath the waist of her panties, finding her folds slick and warm with her need. He let out a soft murmur, reveling in the feel of her, and she gasped when he teased her clit. He repeated the stroke, enjoying her pleasure. He could be domineering, but he didn't want to torment Persia. He wanted to give her something she'd remember.

He stroked her pussy, teasing her slit with sensuous strokes as he familiarized himself with the landscape of her folds. He slipped a finger into her sheath and curled it ever so slightly. She shuddered in his caress—one hand going to her breast while the other clung to the sleeping bag and held tightly. A second, thick finger joined the first and he massaged her pussy, stroke after stroke.

He withdrew and brought his fingers to her clit, the bundle of nerves swollen and so very responsive to his touch. He made small circles with his fingers and she squirmed against him, pushing her ass snugly against his groin. When she whimpered and shuddered once again, he knew he'd found the golden spot. He grew more aggressive, rubbing her with a steady, unrelenting rhythm that had her panting and mewling for more.

He knew she grew closer to release, could sense her rising pleasure and that she rode the edge of orgasm. He could smell it on the air. Practically taste the clouds of bliss. His fingers grew wetter by the moment and Warren wished he'd already had the werewolf talk with her. He wanted to slide into her wet, willing pussy. Sink deeply and fill her with his—

A sound filtered through his desire, an odd sound, one that shouldn't have been. A rope sliding through a carabiner. Warren froze, listening hard to make sure he hadn't imagined it. Persia's panting nearly drowned it out when it happened again, but he heard it. Clear as a bell. A human was messing around at the base of their tree!

Before his poor dearest even knew what was happening, he was out of the sleeping bag and peering over the edge of their treehouse. Then a scent even more powerful than Persia's arousal hit him like a baseball bat.

Human.

Male.

Gunpowder.

Persia eased up next to his tense body, her fingers slipping between his. His wolf surged against Warren's self-control, demanding to be released so he could protect their mate, but Warren only allowed it to come out just enough to boost his vision. No sense overreacting until he was sure there was actually a threat.

Sure enough, a man with a gun slung over his shoulder inched his way up the tree using their own damn climbing ropes.

Fuck!

CHAPTER FOURTEEN

Persia's heart pounded like a tribal drum in her chest, her stomach twisting into knots of anxiety as she peered over the edge of the platform. How could things have changed so quickly? From sleeping as peacefully as she ever had to waking up in the most delightful manner to staring into the abyss, trying to see the threat that had put Warren on high alert. Tension pulsed off him so powerfully it felt like a blazing fire and kept growing, yet she couldn't make out what he seemed to sense.

"What is it?" she whispered, eyes wide as she willed them to adjust to the darkness.

Warren released her hand as she blinked hard again and again, straining to focus on something… *anything*. A small movement caught her attention, and that did it. Suddenly the shape of someone pulling themselves up the tree resolved, and her blood ran cold. It came as such a surprise that she stumbled backward a step and clapped her hands over her mouth so she wouldn't scream.

"Shit!" she hissed, spinning around to see if Warren might have smuggled a cauldron of molten lava in with his supplies so they could pour it over their assailant. But instead she was met with a sight more horrifying, more incomprehensible than she'd ever seen in her life.

"W-warren?" Her throat clamped up, not allowing her to make so much as a squeak after that.

He was no longer the gentle country boy with the soft kisses and the lilting twang as sweet as honey fresh from the hive. The Caribbean blue eyes that melted her to the core intensified to a wholly inhuman shade of cobalt, flashing with rage, even as the structure of his face changed. At first subtly, but then quickly and dramatically. The rest of his body soon followed suit.

No matter how fast or how much she blinked, this bizarre nightmare or vision or whatever it was didn't fade away. It remained, and only became freakier. But it couldn't be real. Not any of it. She had to be dreaming or sleepwalking.

Time slowed as Warren's body bulged and twisted, stretching the seams of his jeans and flannel shirt. He fell onto all fours, his mouth and nose seeming to elongate into a snout—she knew it was impossible, but it was the only way to describe it—and golden fur sprouted over every inch of exposed skin. It must have only taken seconds, but hours seemed to pass as Persia watched, utterly paralyzed as his shirt and pants tore away from his body in shreds, like the Hulk. Except, instead of turning into Lou Ferrigno covered in green makeup, she was left facing something so incomprehensible, her knees gave out and she dropped to her ass, staring at the beast in total, overriding shock.

"Nonononono," she babbled as her brain short-circuited.

Scrambling backward and pressing herself against the rough bark of the tree trunk, she gaped at the huge wolf standing in the middle of the platform, its lips pulled back in a vicious snarl. At least it wasn't snarling at her. The animal's murderous gaze focused on the edge of the platform, where the person climbing the tree would soon appear.

Persia's breaths came in short, quick gasps, her brain frantically trying to make sense of what it had just seen—was *still* seeing—but it couldn't. Instead, it tried to convince her Warren hadn't just turned into a wolf. That the wolf had never been a man to begin with. A man was a man, a wolf was a wolf. Of course, that had to be true, yet… she'd watched Warren change, contort, transform. And she couldn't ignore the fact he was nowhere to be seen. She even craned her neck back to see if he'd climbed the tree, but he'd vanished into thin air.

Maybe he was never here to begin with, her inner pragmatist whispered. Maybe she'd simply dreamed cuddling up with him, kissing him, touching him. Maybe that's what happened.

Then where did the wolf come from? another part of her argued. She hated that part. A bear *might* have climbed a tree, but wolves weren't known for their tree-climbing skills.

I've lost my mind, she decided. It was the only explanation, unless aliens had transported her to an alternate reality or parallel universe or different dimension or whatever the Sci-fi nuts called it. Damn, she was even babbling inside her own head!

The line between reality and hallucination blurred into the background of her mind. Everything was real and nothing was real, all at the same time. With a start, Persia realized Wolf Woods had gone silent. No rustling of foraging nocturnal animals. No birds flitting around as they prepared for the day. Not even the breeze that had cooled her heated skin moments earlier whispered among the leaves. No sound whatsoever from the forest itself, as if it silenced itself to better hear the maelstrom that was about to be unleashed.

Only a few sounds passed the thundering of her heart. The beast—whether imaginary or terrifyingly real—prowled at the edge of the platform, moving silently, even as drool splattered on the freshly cut plywood. Her breaths continued in hot, ragged bursts, and she wondered for a moment if her throat was closing up. Maybe dying like that would be for the best before the wolf could turn its gaze on her. The rough hiss of rope brushing rope reminded her of the threat about to present itself.

Unable to stop herself, she turned her nearly catatonic gaze toward the edge of the platform in time to see a pair of big, strong hands grip the railing Warren had installed just hours earlier. She didn't need to see the man's face to know he was one of her father's hired guns. He'd come for her. Or maybe the massive wolf standing in front of her, shielding her from the hunter. Knowing the tenacity of the men Dick McNish hired, whatever was about to go down, it would not go down easily.

The wolf took a half-step backward, closer to Persia, but somehow, she knew it wasn't because it was afraid. It just wanted to stay out of the hunter's sightline for as long as possible. It was smart. Smarter than an average wolf because the tactic worked. The hunter grunted softly as he hoisted the top half of his body past the edge of the platform and faced them.

The man probably barely had time for his brain to process what it was seeing before the wolf lunged forward, snapping his powerful jaws and latching onto something so hard the crunch made her cringe. The silence of the forest was shattered by a bellow of surprise and pain.

Then the crack of branches and sickening thud of a body hitting the forest floor nearly brought up her beer and potato chips.

Persia held her breath, not daring to move or make a sound. Even though she knew the man had almost certainly been sent to drag her down from the platform, if not kill her outright, she didn't want anyone to die. Silence dragged out for so long she was either going to take a big gasp or pass out, but before either happened, some very colorful curses reached her ears.

Daring to edge closer to the wolf, she peeked down to see the hunter hobbling away from the rabid wolf in the tree and toward the entrance of the woods, holding one hand to his shoulder and dragging a near useless leg behind him.

Once the man was out of sight, the normal night sounds of the woods peppered the air, and Persia dared to face the wolf. Of the many ways she'd envisioned herself dying—skydiving over the Mojave, hiking through the Amazon, hell...driving down I-75 during rush hour—becoming wolf-chow had never been one of them.

But when the animal's bright blue eyes found hers, the fire that had blazed in them moments before winked out and they looked almost familiar. Only when he sat back on his haunches did it hit her. She knew this wolf. Very well.

"Y-you?" she muttered, her heart stuttering in her chest.

The wolf tilted his head to the side and slapped his fluffy tail on the plywood a couple of times, as if asking her a question. Anger surged inside her, drawn from her confusion and fear, as well as relief at knowing her mysterious visitor.

"What the ever-living-*fuck* is going on here!" she shouted, drowning out the night sounds of the woods again. "I'm having a psychotic break. That has to be it. None of this is actually happening. Nope. No way. Nuh-uh. I'm nuts."

People who have psychotic breaks don't usually know they're having them, though, that asshole voice in her head reminded her. Which could only mean one thing.

It was all real.

Tears streamed unbidden down her cheeks and she knew her head was shaking back and forth frantically, although she hadn't specifically told it to. The wolf, her special friend who'd been nothing but kind to her, took a step closer and whined, almost as if it was worried about her. That's all it took to send her into hysterics.

"Get away!" she screamed at him, pushing her back against the trunk like maybe she could somehow bury herself inside to stay safe.

The wolf froze, and then something even crazier happened, confirming she was, in fact, losing her marbles. His furry body lengthened and contorted, his muscled shoulders shrinking and broadening at the same time.

Thick fur retracted as if being sucked back inside by an invisible vacuum, leaving only smooth, tanned skin behind. The still-frothing muzzle shortened back into a human face while his eyes dulled to a mesmerizing, handsome, terrifyingly familiar blue.

The wolf disappeared, replaced by a stark-naked Warren.

"It's okay, Persia," he spoke softly, holding his palms up at her, as if that would somehow make everything better. "Stay calm. You're safe."

It's okay? Stay calm? Bullshit! *Nothing* was okay, so she wasn't about to stay calm. Every cell in her body screamed at her to *run!* Get away from this insanity as fast as she could, *however* she could. Scrambling away from him toward the other side of the platform, she stood and glanced around wildly for her best chance of escape. She had to get out of the tree. Now!

Crouching low and leaping with every ounce of strength she possessed, Persia managed to wrap her hands around the next closest branch, adrenaline masking the deep gouges the rough bark left on her fingers. Pain-schmain. She wasn't above free-climbing this bitch of a tree, and she sure as hell wasn't going to wait around to be gobbled up by some human-wolf mutant, no matter how sweet and cute and sexy as hell he was when he was being sweet and cute. Nuh-uh, no way.

Holding her breath, Persia pulled with all her might, swinging one leg up toward the branch but missing by a mile. She dangled from her branch, a good thirty feet over the forest floor, struggling to stay out of Warren's reach, when her vision began to blur. Her limbs felt as heavy as logs and she could barely keep her eyes open. Dizziness overcame her, and the last thing she knew was the terrifying sensation of falling.

CHAPTER FIFTEEN

"ALL RIGHT," ZEKE GROANED, RUNNING HIS HANDS OVER HIS face in Trina's clinic a few hours later. "Can we go over again how we got from 'a hunter at the base of the tree' to 'our attorney lying in a clinic'?"

Warren paced Trina's small clinic with a snow lion flag that read *Free Tibet!* wrapped around his waist in lieu of clothing. His sister bent over an unconscious Persia, opening her eyelids and shining a light in them, checking for a concussion. *Another* concussion, he reminded himself.

What a shit show!

"He knew we were up there," Warren grumbled, out of patience with his alpha's multitude of questions. He was right to be asking them, but that didn't mean Warren had the patience to answer them. "If I hadn't woken up, the bastard would have gotten the drop on us."

No one else needed to know the hunter had interrupted a hot-and-heavy make-out session, which only brought back memories of how Persia's body had reacted to his touch, his kiss. Her soft sighs, his overpowering need for her.

Val snapped her fingers in front of Warren's face. "Snap out of it, loverboy. Now explain why you shifted in front of her. And let me remind you of the seriousness of that particular offense."

Ironic, coming from Val, considering her mate's sister had shifted in front of her when they were college roommates.

"I had no choice," Warren snapped, watching Trina's every movement. "It was one of McNish's hunters. I'd bet my life on it. He knew exactly where we were, he was sneaking up on us, and he had a gun. Honestly, I think that's what woke up my wolf. I never would have smelled the gunpowder on my own, but he was close to the surface."

Zeke raised a curious eyebrow, but Warren ignored him in favor of keeping his focus on his mate.

"I wasn't about to risk my mate's safety, Zeke, and I know you would have done the same. Lucky for the hunter, he didn't make it as close as my wolf wanted." He shrugged his disinterest over the hunter's fate. "My fangs probably didn't even puncture the skin, but I might have cracked his clavicle. I think the fall really hurt him. Not so badly he couldn't hobble away pretty fast, though. Bottom line, he'll live."

"Okay," Zeke frowned at his beta. "Did he see you shift?"

"Not a chance. As far as he knows, some crazy wolf somehow managed to climb a tree. Unless McNish filled his goons in on the truth, I doubt anyone will take him seriously. Just another fictitious Wolf Woods sighting that will feed local lore."

"What about Persia?" Zeke's hard gaze bore into him.

"She saw the whole thing. After the hunter fell, she flipped her shit and tried to climb the tree to get away from me. I can't really blame her. It's not how I envisioned telling her. It must have overwhelmed her because she passed out mid-climb. I managed to catch her before she could fall."

After lowering her limp body to the platform, Warren had harnessed her in and then used the belaying lines he'd used for the supplies to lower them both to the ground, grabbing her Tibet flag on the way, just in case he ran into anyone. He'd then carried her all the way across Wolf Woods and pack lands to Trina's cabin-slash-clinic. Heading to his truck would have been too risky.

"How is she?" he dared ask his sister.

Trina smiled and gave his shoulder a squeeze before pulling the stethoscope's ear tips out of her ears. "I'm pretty sure she just fainted, big brother. She should be fine. That was quick thinking on your part. I think you saved her life more than once tonight. Or last night. What time is it again?"

"Five," Max growled hoarsely as he walked into the clinic from the cabin and handed his mate a mug of steaming Earl Grey tea. She pecked his cheek, and then he took one look at a nearly naked Warren before disappearing back into the cabin.

Maybe he should have been relieved at the diagnosis, but his sister's equivocation troubled him. "You're sure? Why hasn't she woken up yet?" he didn't even try to hide the worry from his voice.

"Warren, she's been through a lot in the last twenty-four hours," Trina chided. "That bump she got the other night might be why. If she hasn't sustained any new injuries, I'm almost certain she'll wake up soon."

"Almost?" he snapped, directing his guilt and worry at the wrong person.

Val moved to step between the siblings, but Trina brushed her aside and gave her brother a hard look. "Listen, Warren, I'm not a human doctor. You know that better than anyone. But I know an injury when I see one, and she has none. So cut the crap, or your ass will be sitting in my waiting room."

She pointed at the clinic's only door, which led directly outside. No way was he going to leave his mate, so he bit his tongue and glowered as his sister did a few more tests. Max wandered back in, glanced down at the flag around his waist, and handed Warren a set of sweats.

"She might not appreciate seeing your junk rubbing up against the symbol of Tibetan liberation when she wakes up." He gave a wry smirk and a wink.

Warren gave him a grateful nod and, as he finished dressing, Persia began to stir. Every head in the room jerked in her direction, and Warren rushed to her side, taking her cool hand in both of his. Zeke and Val flanked him while Trina remained on her other side.

Her eyes fluttered open and then squinted against the bright light of the clinic. When her eyes adjusted a little, her gaze skimmed over those clustered around her, landing on Warren. Her hand tightened around his for a moment, driving home the knowledge she was his and he was hers. A whisper of a smile played at her lips, the same kind of sleepy look she'd given him when she awoke on the platform.

Then her eyes widened, and her pupils dilated. Sweet affection gave way to terror. All color drained from her face and her chest expanded in preparation for a bloodcurdling scream. The moment her piercing shriek ruptured the air, all hell broke loose.

Persia flailed around, trying to scramble away from the source of her panic—Warren. Val's instincts presumably kicked in as she tried to keep Persia on the gurney, as Trina and Warren used soothing tones to try to calm her down. Zeke shouted for Max to get his ass over and help while Max backed away from the chaos, which Warren appreciated. He wasn't crazy about Val touching his mate. If another male—mated or not—touched her, he might go nuts.

"Persia, honey, you need to calm down or you'll pass out again," Trina remained firm, her voice just this side of shouting.

"Calm the fuck down," Val growled as she struggled to restrain her without hurting her.

"You're safe, Persia," Warren tried on a smile, but she only cringed away from him.

"Take some deep breaths," Zeke added with an authoritative tone that certainly didn't soothe Warren's nerves, and he doubted it would help Persia.

"You guys, maybe you should—" Max started, but Trina cut him off with a look.

Warren was desperate to help her, to calm her down, to show her they meant no harm, but she couldn't hear them over her own screams. "I said you're safe," he raised his voice. "Everything's okay!"

"Warren, you're not helping," Val barked.

"Neither are you. Let her go!"

Trina scowled at them all. "Everyone needs to shut—"

A cool blast of early morning air hit them all, carrying with it the scent of the pack omega, Cassandra. She drifted in like a leaf on the wind, her power radiating out from her and soothing all but Persia's jangled nerves. She didn't even need to utter a single word to get everyone to take a couple of steps away from the patient. She simply glided over to them, her snow-white hair billowing down the length of her back and blending perfectly with her equally white silk gown. Leaning over a still-babbling Persia, she smiled, and the room filled with a peaceful warmth.

"Good morning, Persia," Cassandra reached out and laid her hand on Persia's cheek.

Persia froze and then sighed and relaxed a little. Her eyes still bugged out and her chest pumped with her panicked breathing, but at least her screams had faded into faint whimpers.

Cassandra's smile grew wider. "You're among friends here, Persia. Deep down you know that. Right?"

Persia's gaze flicked toward Warren and then back to Cassandra, and she gave a tiny nod that blasted him with hope.

"Good," Cassandra continued. "Your friends are going to tell you everything you want to know about them. All you need to do is take a deep breath and keep an open mind. I promise, no one will hurt you. Do you believe me?"

Her nod was more emphatic that time. Then her disarming blue-brown gaze landed on him again, and Cassandra took a step back to allow him to approach. Persia looked as confused as ever. He just hoped he could explain everything without scaring her again. Scratching at the back of his neck, he took a deep breath and dove right in.

"I'm so sorry for frightening you like that, Persia, but I only did it to protect you. Before you ask, yes, what you saw really happened. I can transform from a human to a wolf. The same wolf you've been visiting in the meadow. I know that must sound crazy to you, but it's true. I can show you again, if you need—"

Persia's eyes grew wide again and Cassandra softly spoke, "I don't think that will be necessary at the moment."

Val moved into Persia's sightline and smiled. "I know exactly how you're feeling, hon. I found out about werewolves the same way you did, totally by accident.

Trust me. What you're feeling right now is completely normal. Just give it a minute."

Persia blinked. "W-werewolves?"

Val exchanged a look with Zeke, who joined her next to the gurney. "All of us 'homesteaders' who live on the mountain? Yeah, we're not actually a village. We're a pack of werewolves. I'm the pack alpha, not the mayor."

Warren perched on the edge of the gurney and clasped her hand again. He was surprised and pleased she didn't pull away. The simple act of touching her helped ease his anxiety, and he hoped somehow their connection helped her too.

"We live among humans, but we keep our true nature a secret. Otherwise they'd all freak out like you did." His lips curled into a gentle smile. "To prevent accidental exposure, we generally live on the outskirts of towns and keep our distance."

"Not always, though," Val interjected. "Zeke's sister was my college roommate in Atlanta. I caught her shifting one day and I'm pretty sure my reaction was similar to yours. We had to have this same chat. By the time I met Zeke, I'd known about wolves for a good decade."

Persia's gaze darted between Val and Zeke. She knew they were a couple, and slowly the dots connected in her brain.

"Does that mean you're..."

Val nodded. "We all are. I'm still kind of a newbie at this whole wolf thing, but I'm getting the hang of it."

Zeke beamed at his mate with pride. "Better than that. You were born to become a wolf, my love."

Val laid a protective hand on her slightly protruding stomach and returned his look of love. "This one too."

Persia focused on Val. "How did you… How did it… How?"

She didn't need to finish her questions for everyone in the room to understand what she wanted to know. They were the obvious questions, the ones anyone in her position would ask. Tougher questions would come later, and Warren was prepared to answer them, but at that moment, the existence of werewolves needed to sink in first.

"Most of us are born as wolves," Warren answered, "though some wolves are made. But don't worry. In our society, it's a death penalty offense for a wolf to turn a human who isn't their fated mate."

Persia's brow crinkled. "Fated what?"

Warren's heart thundered. How would she react to what he had to tell her? The idea of losing her was almost too much to bear, but he had no other choice. She needed to know everything.

"Fated mates. Love works a little differently for us, Persia. Wolves mate for life, and we find each other by smell. The moment a wolf catches the scent of his fated mate, something changes inside him. Only his mate matters, above everything else except for the pack, for the rest of his life."

Persia stared at him intently, a question bouncing around in her eyes. Then she swallowed hard and gave it voice. "Do *you* have a mate?"

Emotion roiled around inside him—how could it not? But instead of trying to hide it, he let it all out for her to see before answering her.

"Sure do, Red. You."

CHAPTER SIXTEEN

Persia's mind buzzed so loudly she couldn't focus on any one thing for longer than a half-second. It was like when you click the wrong link on your computer and your screen fills with dozens upon dozens of annoying pop-ups. Only her brain was the screen and the crazy tale these seemingly sane people were telling her were the pop-ups. If only one tiny aspect made sense, maybe the pain behind her eyes would stop.

She pinched the bridge of her nose and squeezed her eyes shut. "I'm sorry, but I'm having a little trouble keeping up."

"That's perfectly understandable," Trina laid a comforting hand on her shoulder.

She probably should have flinched at the touch of a lunatic, but it somehow grounded her.

"What don't you understand?" Warren asked in a perfectly courteous tone that somehow irritated her.

"Oh, I dunno, let's see… I don't understand anything at all about magical creatures who can turn themselves from humans to wolves. Not even a little bit, outside the context of a bad horror flick. Another thing I don't understand is this fated whatever concept. I mean, don't get me wrong, it's every girl's fantasy to have a man fall for her so hard he'd become her lover and protector for the rest of their lives, but…gimme a break. Life doesn't work that way."

It all had to be some kind of epic gag, maybe some new reality show pranking unsuspecting women with promises of eternal love. Cruel, but the world had become a truly cruel place.

"It does," Warren insisted, a strange desperation flickering across his face. "I swear—"

"Okay, assuming werewolves are real, which I don't believe for a second, I'm not one. How could I possibly be your mate?" She used air quotes around "mate."

"Don't forget, I was human too," Val chimed in. "I thought all this fated mate stuff was just a bunch of hooey at first. But I can tell you, Persia, I wouldn't have it any other way. The truth of the matter is that I never felt like I fit in anywhere until I landed here. Not when I was on the Dean's List in college, not when I was making a name for myself in the Army, not even in combat, which I'd always thought was my true calling."

Persia wanted to pepper her with questions, but giving voice to those thoughts might suggest she believed one tiny iota of what they were saying.

Which she didn't.

Nope.

Not at all.

"I will admit that when I first met Zeke, I felt nothing but a strong attraction." Zeke scowled at this and glanced around the room, silently telling everyone to keep that bit of information to themselves. "True, it was stronger than anything I'd ever felt, but I wouldn't call it life-changing. It felt a bit like if you were to stick a fork in an electrical outlet. You'd get a little singed, maybe fall on your ass, and you'd definitely think, 'What the fuck just happened?' But now that I'm a shifter, I can tell you that feeling is intensified, more like grabbing a downed power line with your bare hand. It's soul-shaking."

That seemed to mollify Zeke because he wrapped an arm around her shoulders and pressed a sweet kiss to her temple.

"Now I *do* belong," Val continued. "I don't just feel it. I know it. I have my mate, my friends, the entire pack, who've become my family. My pack mates accept and love me for who I am, potty mouth and all. I'm not going to lie. It's hard to wrap your mind around, but all I can tell you is that I feel complete now. Like I've found my place in the universe. And since I no longer have to search for it, I can relax and enjoy every second of it."

Val's speech really hit home with Persia. She'd always felt out of place. Growing up, she'd been a tomboy when her mother had wanted her to be a girly girl. Her father had hoped she'd follow in his footsteps, which she clearly hadn't. Even the only people she could come close to calling friends were transitory—and most of them were sitting in jail cells at that moment, no doubt hating her guts. The thought of finally belonging somewhere appealed to Persia more than she ever would have imagined. Maybe…

"No, no, no." She shook her red curls hard enough they bounced against her face. "Stop messing with me, you guys."

"Do you need proof?" Max stepped close enough for her to see him. "I'd be happy to show you how it's done."

Trina's husband—or mate or whatever he was called—started unbuttoning his shirt, which drew a growl from Warren. Dragging Max out of Persia's field of vision, he stepped in to take his place.

"If anyone's going to shift in front of my mate, it's going to be me!"

Spotty memories of Warren's body transforming into some kind of mutant creature shot adrenaline through her veins, ratcheting up her heart rate. The terror she'd felt staring into his wild, glowing eyes thirty feet up a tree…which wasn't real. Couldn't be. Yet no matter how hard she tried to believe it had all been a dream, she couldn't erase the images of Warren's transformation from her mind. She'd been there. She'd seen it. Proof of what they all claimed.

"No, don't do that shifty thing." She covered her eyes as if he might do it anyway. "I've already seen that show. Twice. I think I've met my quota for a lifetime."

Trina squeezed her shoulder. "Trust your instincts, Persia. Listen to them, even if your rational brain tries to convince you otherwise."

Tears burned the backs of her eyes as she tried to make sense of it all. She couldn't deny what she saw on that platform, and all of her instincts screamed that her new friends were telling the truth. But still…

"Hey, I have a thought." Warren pulled her hand to help her sit up. "Why don't I show you around, give you a little tour of the pack house? You could get a sense of who we are as a community. No pressure, nothing scary, I promise."

"Is she okay to walk around?" Val murmured to Trina.

"Sure, just take it easy. No long hikes in the woods, and definitely no more falling down again, okay?"

Persia thought for a moment. Everyone in the room exuded thoughtfulness and caring, so she had no reason to think they were setting her up. Besides, a walk sounded nice after the night she'd had. She nodded her agreement, and then Trina turned to Warren.

"I'm serious, Warren. You need to keep a close eye on her. Agreed?"

Warren's expression grew steely, and then he uttered a single word that caused the breath in her throat to catch. "Always."

The double meaning of that word wasn't lost on her, but she couldn't unpack what it all meant just then. Slipping to the ground, she reached for Warren's proffered arm. The moment her hand tucked into the crook of his elbow, a current of what felt like electricity pulsed through her body. Like, real, knock-you-out-of-your-shoes electricity. Exactly as Val had described it. Pushing the thought from her mind, she focused on putting each foot in front of the other until they closed in on a large log cabin structure.

"This is the pack house," Warren explained, as a few people—no wolves—stood on the big wrap-around porch drinking steaming cups of coffee. "Zeke and Val live there full-time, as well as a handful of other pack members. The rest of us have small homes on pack lands, and a few even live in Tremble. In general, we prefer everyone to live on pack lands because it's safer, but it's not required."

"Why is it safer?"

"Don't get me wrong, Tremble is a nice town, and most of the locals are good people. But out here, we're hidden from prying eyes and the dangers inherent with humans discovering our existence."

"Like my dad."

It wasn't a question because it made sense. Assuming all of it was true. Which it wasn't. Couldn't be.

"I wasn't… I didn't mean…" Warren stammered, clearly worried he'd offended her.

She gave him a glum smirk. "I know you didn't. But it's the truth. Men like my dad are why you feel the need to hide." She left out the part about his community's shared delusions.

"Packs are structured much like the military, with a specific hierarchy and strong leadership. We're all wolves, but we're not all equal. The Ruling Circle consists of the alpha as the leader, his beta as a sort of right-hand man, and an enforcer who commands the security force, who are called sentries. Is that too much detail?"

"No, I'm picking up what you're laying down," she responded as she caught sight of a small van waiting a short distance from the pack house. "Do you have a position in the… pack?"

A proud smile touched his lips. "I'm Zeke's beta, second in command."

"Do you ever wish *you* were the leader?" Most guys saw themselves as alphas, even though most guys weren't.

"Good lord, no." He chuckled. "That's an immense amount of pressure, and despite being new to the job, Zeke's handling it all really well. We each have our own calling. Val is unique—well, in a lot of ways, but especially because she's not only the alpha mate, a position that offers a lot of power in itself, but she's also the pack's enforcer. Trina's innate healing abilities make her the perfect healer, and Cassandra…well, Cassandra is a natural born omega."

"You mean the beautiful, white-haired woman who came in? What's an omega?"

Warren nodded as they rounded the front porch on their lazy stroll. "It's hard to explain, but the best I can tell you is that she's a sort of mystic, or psychic healer, if that sounds better."

None of it sounded better. In fact, the whole thing was getting weirder and weirder.

"Yeah, that doesn't sound fake at all. Although, I have to admit, I calmed down pretty fast once she walked in."

"That's part of her role as omega."

"What about you, Warren? Becoming a beta is your *raison d'être?*"

He stopped dead in his tracks, and she stumbled a few extra steps before turning to face him. What she saw in his eyes scared her. Not in a "I'm about to gobble you up, Little Red Riding Hood" way, but in a "Oh shit, he ain't playing" kind of way. The way he looked at her flooded her body with heat and need. She almost wished they were back in the treehouse, making out like teenagers.

"No, Persia, it's not my reason for being. I thought it was, for a long time, but then I caught your scent in Wolf Woods. I waited for you, you know. I smelled you long before I saw you, or even heard your progress. When you stepped out into the clearing, the sun glinted off your hair like it was on fire. My wolf wanted to run to you, but I told him that would scare you. So, we waited. And you came to us. You laid down with us, bared your soul to us. That was when I learned my purpose in life. To be the best damn mate possible."

The morning bustle going on around them vanished as Persia stared up at him, blinking rapidly as she tried to process his words into something that made sense. It didn't work. The only explanation for him knowing all of that was that…

"It *was* you! You really *are* my woodland friend!"

Part of her felt faint, but another part of her felt excited and joyful and happier than she ever thought possible. Then the reality of it all erased her fledgling smile and replaced it with a frown.

"What?" he asked, peering at her with an intensity that felt almost invasive.

"I dunno, Warren. That seems so… tricky. How can I trust you? You should have told me who—or rather *what*—you are."

The intensity softened and he quirked an eyebrow at her. "You mean like how you should have told me you were Dick McNish's daughter?"

Persia winced and gave him a sheepish grimace. "Touché."

He tucked her hand back into the crook of his arm and continued their walk, his warm fingers covering her trembling ones. "Besides, considering your reaction to *what* I am, I'm sure you can understand why I didn't mention it sooner."

Vaguely recalling the sheer panic she'd felt the night before and the ear-splitting screams she'd belted out a short time earlier, she had to give him that. "Fair enough."

A tiny blur of tan and orange tore across the lawn toward them, and Persia wondered what fresh hell was coming at her now. As the creature slowed to run circles around them, she realized it was just a dog. A very small Pomeranian, if she wasn't mistaken.

Warren laughed and crouched low to allow the pooch to jump in his arms. "Persia, I'd like you to meet another member of our pack, Fang. Fang, meet Persia."

Fang stretched herself as far as she could to reach Persia without leaving Warren's arms. Persia scratched the little dog's ear and moved in close enough for a few puppy kisses. "Nice to meet you, Fang."

Having properly greeted their guest, the dog leapt from Warren's arms and tore off to god knew where, leaving Persia amused at the presence of a dog in a supposed wolf pack. But before she could ask about it, a familiar, gruff voice called out to her.

"Morning, Persia!"

Turning, she watched her boss, Hux Davenport, hurrying across the lawn toward them, a small boy with matching features riding on his shoulders. He smiled as they passed and headed for the waiting van.

What.

The.

Hell?

She turned surprised eyes on Warren. "He's…?"

Warren grinned. "Yup. He's taking Little Hux to the van that will drive them to school in town. After what that poor kid's been through, Hux makes a point of escorting him every morning now."

Too much information had already filled up her brain. She feared there wasn't enough room for more, so she didn't ask what the boy had suffered through. Even if she had, her question would have been drowned out by the sound of several more little ones shouting and laughing and generally being excited kids, all heading for the same van. One actually shifted into a tiny wolf pup, mid-stride, leaving a pile of clothes behind.

"What the..." she gasped, shocked to see a human shift in the light of day. It was much as she remembered from the night before, but much less terrifying and infinitely cuter. And so very real.

Warren chuckled softly. "His mom's going to give him a time out for ruining his school clothes, for sure."

The children were funny, but the adults running in circles as they tried to herd the hyper kids into the van drew a chuckle from Persia. Even Hux chased after his son, his mini-me giggling as he tried to evade his papa. Meanwhile, tiny little Fang yipped and chased after everyone.

The terror she'd felt that morning melted away entirely. This was just a community, like any other. Well, not *quite* like any other, but close enough. People who cared and watched out for each other, loving families just trying to get by, folks who just wanted to live their lives without being gunned down on their own land.

"I can't wait," Warren murmured as he stared wistfully at the scene.

"For what?"

"To have some pups of our own."

Cue record scratch.

Pulling her hand back, she stared at him like…well, like he'd just said he wanted to have *pups* with her.

Pups!

"Excuse me?"

He turned a perplexed look on her. "What?"

"You want to have *what* with me?"

"Pups. Don't you want kids?"

Could he really be that dense? "Whether I do or not, I literally found out just minutes ago that an unknown number of humans can turn themselves into fucking *werewolves* at will, and quite honestly, I'm having a hard enough time wrapping my head around *that*. Then you dump this crazy 'fated mate' thing on me, and now you already have me barefoot and pregnant with wolf babies? You seriously need to slow your roll, Bubba. Big time."

"I just—" he stammered for a moment, seemingly blown away by her hesitancy. "I just thought now that you knew the truth, you'd understand. That you'd want the claiming bite that will turn you into a wolf and bond us together for eternity."

Persia snorted, staring at up at the sky in complete disbelief. "You hear yourself. Right? Tell me you hear how crazy that all sounds."

"Not to me."

His eyes glittered earnestly, and for a moment a vision of them doddering through their golden years with dozens of grandchildren running circles around them brought a wave of joy to her heart. But then her brain started working again.

"Warren, come on. That's not how things work. It's a pretty idea, but it's just not what happens in the real world. You know what does? Marriages like my parents'. He's a workaholic who ignores his wife and probably sleeps around on business trips. She's a spoiled trophy wife who spends all her time—and her husband's money —on trips around the world, probably also sleeping around the whole way. That's what a *real* marriage looks like. Boredom. Loneliness. Resentment. Distance. I don't want that for myself, Warren. What I want is to stop my father, and that's exactly what I'm going to do."

If she didn't get out of there, her brain might explode. Without thinking about it first, Persia broke away from Warren and hurried up the steps to the school van just as the driver closed the door. The man gave her a curious look but then shrugged and drove away from what Warren had called the pack house.

Taking a seat next to Little Hux in the front row, Persia did her best not to look back. If she did, she might change her mind and ask the driver to let her out. But her gaze didn't seem to want to obey her command. Turning in her seat, she stared out the back window and her heart cracked in two.

Warren stood alone in the billowing dust, watching helplessly as she was whisked away.

CHAPTER SEVENTEEN

WARREN STOOD FROZEN IN PLACE LONG AFTER THE VAN carrying Persia had disappeared from sight. Even the dust had settled. All the parents had dispersed to go about their daily business, not paying attention to the heartbroken beta watching his mate run from him. Only Fang remained, sitting near his feet. She craned her tiny neck to watch him and whined softly at his distress, but he barely noticed her.

"Good morning again, Warren," sang a melodic voice he recognized immediately.

Cassandra had a knack for sneaking up on people, though no one suspected that was her intent. She also had a habit of showing up at either the most or least convenient times. Warren had no doubt *that* was deliberate.

For the first time he could recall, Cassandra's presence didn't have a calming effect on him. Fang stopped whining, but his heart continued to ache. When she caught sight of his face, a whisper of a wrinkle formed between her eyebrows where most adults had deeply etched worry lines.

"I take it your tour didn't go as well as you'd hoped," she spoke softly, placing a hand on his shoulder.

Nothing. Not a warming glow spreading through his body. Not even a glimmer of Cassandra's power could pass through his pain. But her presence did give him an idea. And *that* allowed a spark of hope to cast a dim light in the darkness.

"Cassandra," he turned to her with desperation in his eyes. "Make her love me."

The pack omega didn't laugh often, but she actually tittered in surprise at his demand. Only once she contained herself did she reply, giving him a sympathetic smile as she realized he'd been serious.

"It doesn't work that way, Warren."

"I saw you do it to that hunter guy, Randy Leeper." He grabbed the hand on his arm and refused to let go. He'd hold on until she made things all better. That was her damn job. "You turned a bloodthirsty hunter into a marshmallow who loves kittens and hugs. It should be a snap to make Persia fall in love with me."

Cassandra sighed, causing that tiny flame of hope to flicker and dim. "First of all, I wasn't even sure my powers would transfer to a human, so I can't say with any certainty how I was able to transform him. But let me assure you, whatever he is now was always waiting just under the surface. All I did was turn his eyes inward, which allowed his true nature to come to the fore. It's my belief that he'd spent years, maybe all of his life, burying that nature under layers of toxic masculinity."

"Then turn Persia's eyes inward so she can see she loves me," he insisted, not willing to give up.

"Oh, my dear Warren. One isn't born with love for someone else. It's created, nurtured, earned. Human love is especially complex since they don't have our ability to detect their mate."

Instead of pulling free from his vice-like grip, she wrapped her other hand around his, clearly trying to give him strength but failing miserably.

"You will have my support in any way I can give it, Warren. A wolf finding his or her mate in a human is… challenging, at best. The wolf must tread carefully and work hard to earn the human's love. It takes far more finesse than simply throwing her over your shoulder and getting to work making pups the minute you meet. That type of behavior is unfathomable to humans. Most wait years for anything remotely close to that, and sometimes it never comes at all."

"But what about Val?" He'd grasp at any straw at this point.

Fang yipped at the sound of her mistress's name and then trotted off toward the pack house to find her. Cassandra gave him a blissful smile.

"Val was a human when she met Zeke, I'll give you that, but she was far from typical. And don't forget she'd had many years to accept our existence. It would be unfair and unkind to compare your situations."

Poof! The ember of hope winked out. Despair gripped him. Releasing Cassandra, he scowled at the dirt.

"Then it's over," he murmured, his voice cracking at the end.

She waited a beat, then offered, "Not necessarily. How have you worked for Persia's love?"

He perked up at that. "I helped get all those treehouses of theirs built, for one. Zeke donated the materials, and a bunch of sentries volunteered to help build them."

"So…you did anything a generous construction worker with the same goal as the protestors might do," she noted dryly.

That didn't sound romantic when she said it that way. "Yeah, but—"

"What else?"

Warren racked his brain. "I, um, worked with my shirt off?"

She seemed wholly unimpressed by that, so he hurriedly came up with something else. "Cassandra, I've shown her everything about myself, what pack life could be like, what our future might be. She knows how I feel and she knows we're mates, but she turned her nose up at all of it. What more can I do?"

Cassandra trailed a ghostly pale finger down his cheek. "My boy, so much more. Can you think of nothing you have in common? Nothing that's connected you on a non-physical plane?"

The it hit him. "Yes! She loves my wolf. Before she... found out about me, I would meet her in the clearing in Wolf Woods in my wolf form. Once she realized I wasn't going to eat her for brunch, she opened up to me, venting about this and that. That's how I got to know her better."

"I see," Cassandra mused, a single eyebrow shooting up in amusement. "Unconventional, and perhaps a little deceptive, but clever. Did you touch her?"

"Of course. As much as I could, anyway."

"Sexually?"

"What? No! Normal stuff, like nuzzling her hand or licking her face, that kind of thing."

"Uh huh," she murmured, as if she were mulling over this information, but Warren sensed she already knew what she was about to say. "And how often do you see humans licking each other's faces?"

His stomach dropped like an old balloon on a cold day.

"Don't look so dejected, Warren. You and your wolf may have different ways of handling your instincts, but you share the same core personality. If she loves your wolf, I believe there's hope she'll grow to love you, if you put in the work."

"What kind of work? Tell me." He'd do anything to win her. *Anything.*

"First you need to find human versions of licking her face. Think about what she likes about your wolf. Besides your fluffy coat," she added with a wink.

Warren had never felt so confused and aimless. He was usually the one with the sage advice, the conservative plan of action. But now he had no idea how to proceed.

"She likes talking to him, I guess, telling him about all the stuff she's dealing with."

"Ah! So, she likes a good listener. When you're in your human form, do you listen with the same attention as your wolf?"

Of course, he wanted to say, though he knew it was a lie. He'd spent plenty of time chatting and trying to impress her.

"I guess I just think that's the sort of things friends do," he muttered, not particularly liking the view in the figurative mirror Cassandra was holding in front of him.

"You don't think mates should be friends too?" she asked with a soft laugh that sent flames to his cheeks. "For humans, friendship usually comes long before love. You want to be her lover immediately, and I understand that impulse. It's in your nature. But it's not in hers, so if you want her, you're going to have to throttle your instincts and cater to hers. Try being her friend, Warren. Only then will you have a chance at winning her heart."

"And if that never happens?"

The smile that always seemed to play at the corners of Cassandra's mouth turned down into a well-defined frown. "Hypotheticals are dangerous, but I won't lie. When a wolf knows who their fated mate is, but for whatever reason can't have them, that poor wolf has my greatest sympathy."

"Why?" he asked, despite his great desire not to. It was always sunny in denial.

"Because that wolf would live the rest of his or her life in abject misery. It's a fate no normal wolf would wish on their worst enemy."

A darkness so black and dense that all hope was gobbled up by its gravity clouded his eyes, heart and soul. He clenched his jaw to keep from sobbing like a child in the middle of the pack house lawn. Capturing Cassandra's gaze with an urgency he felt all the way to the tips of his hair, he took a step toward her.

"Then take it from me now."

"Take… what?"

"The mate thing. The drive, the connection, whatever it is. I don't care if that means I'll be alone for the rest of my life. I can't imagine a lifetime of this pain. Just do your voodoo and make it so she's not my mate. I mean, she's human. It can't be that hard."

The look of pity and disappointment in her eyes shamed Warren more than words ever could. Then came her words.

"Warren, I love you as much as any other member of this pack, so I'm going to speak frankly. If you would rather ask for magic that would take away any chance at joy in your future than work for the love of your mate, then Persia isn't the problem here. You are. To quote a human colloquialism, shit or get off the pot."

Rage and shame forced him to turn his back on the omega and stomp off in a huff. He'd *tried* to make Persia fall in love with him, but where did that get him? Nowhere, that's where. So, he'd just spend his life wrapped in misery so heavy it would eventually drag him down like an anchor. He'd been the pack's sad sack for years now anyway. Who would even notice the difference?

Just as he entered the forest, he stopped in his tracks, his jaw set.

Unless...

CHAPTER EIGHTEEN

A HEAVY SILENCE LAY OVER THE PREVIOUSLY BUSTLING protest site at the entrance to Wolf Woods. Persia sat hunched over the tiny fold-out table in Betty, triple-checking every piece of paperwork for any mistakes. It all needed to be perfect if she had a chance of winning a temporary injunction against her father. One misspelling could get her motion thrown out of court, leaving him free to proceed with his plans to start tearing down the woods.

After hitching a ride in the van taking all those cute kids to school, Persia had slipped the driver ten bucks to drop her at Wolf Woods so she could finalize her paperwork and head to the courthouse. As urgent as the injunction was, though, she continually caught herself staring out the side window of her van toward the woods. More specifically, toward the meadow in the woods. Clear morning light streamed through the trees in pillars of pale gold. Birds did their birdy things, as if they hadn't a care in the world. Far too much beauty and bliss for her state of mind, so she returned her gaze to the documents and tried not to think about Warren and werewolves and adorable kids who could shift into even more adorable puppies.

The sound of gravel crunching under tires brought her back to reality. For a brief moment, her heart leapt at the thought Warren had followed her, but one glance out her back window killed that fantasy. Her father's BMW pulled up directly behind her, as if she needed yet one more dark cloud to fuck up an already grim day.

"Shit," she muttered, gathering up all her paperwork and shoving it in a folder.

Sliding open the side door and jumping out, she quickly closed and locked the van, just in case. Considering he'd sent one of his hunters to either kidnap or kill her the night before, it didn't pay to take chances.

"Morning, princess," Dick flashed a warm grin, as if they weren't bitter enemies.

"What do you want?" Her hostile tone left nothing to the imagination.

Dick held his hands up in surrender. "I come in peace," he teased, but Persia no longer trusted any of his tones. "Honestly, I was hoping we could talk."

Oh, that didn't sound suspicious as hell. "About what?"

"Isn't it obvious?" he asked simply.

It was. She glanced at the folder inside Betty and then nodded. "Fine, talk."

"It's a perfect morning for taking a walk with your ol' dad," he offered his arm.

She ignored it and set off toward the clearing, partly out of habit, but more in hopes he'd see the beauty of the place and decide to leave it undisturbed. A long shot, no doubt about it, but it sure as hell couldn't hurt.

He quickly fell behind, concerned over low shrubs catching his suit pants or scuffing his polished shoes. Persia continued to trudge along, taking sour pleasure in his discomfort. Once the path cleared a bit, he managed to reach her side.

"You wanted to talk, so talk," she grumbled, keeping her gaze on the terrain.

"Well, quite frankly, I miss you."

This stunned her so savagely she stopped abruptly and stared at him as if he'd grown a second head. His grey eyes were shaded, almost guarded. And not because his heart was on the line. The man didn't have one, so he obviously had other motives. She snorted, rolled her eyes and got back to walking.

"Uh huh, sure. You almost had me there for a second."

He hurried to catch up again. "It's true. Your mother misses you too."

This time she laughed outright. "Oh, please. Mother barely even knows I exist. I want you to guess the last time I heard from her. Go ahead, guess."

They trudged along for a moment before he guessed, "Your birthday?"

Persia didn't bother trying to stop her bitter laughter. "Well, technically you're right, but I'll give you a bonus question. *Which* birthday?"

"Uh…"

"My twenty-fifth, Daddy. Three years ago." She sighed heavily. "Listen, I don't hold it against her. You can correct me if I'm wrong, but she never wanted a kid in the first place. Trust me. She doesn't miss me."

"Now, princess—"

"Give it up already. It's not like either of you really had a hand in raising me. That was left to the plethora of nannies that came and went, even when Mom *wasn't* off being slathered in suntan lotion by some cute cabaña boy in a foreign land."

The not-so-subtle accusation of her mother's probable infidelity didn't even make her father flinch. "Well, I still miss you."

"Oh, please. You don't even know me."

It was her father's turn to snort. "I know you better than you think. You're my daughter, my blood."

"Sadly."

Tension buzzed between them as they trudged along. Persia didn't *hate* her father. She hated what he did, which probably meant she should hate him, but he was still her father. They'd had poignant moments and a handful of happy memories together. Still, she knew they'd never have a healthy relationship.

"You're too smart for your own good," Dick said softly. "You think you're always right and know better than everyone else. You're stubborn as a mule. You're a romantic at heart, even though you probably think you're a stoic. But worst of all, you truly believe good will always triumph over evil."

"And that's a bad thing?"

"It's… misguided, and you know it. You're smart enough to know the world isn't black and white, good and bad. That's all just a construct devised to keep the proletariat under control. There are only varying shades of grey, my dear."

Persia's mind instantly flashed on a certain book she and all her girlfriends had read back in college. It made her think of sex, which made her think about Warren's perfect, muscular body. Which led to remembering how gently he'd caressed her, the sweetness of his kiss, the heat of his desire. None of which should have crossed her mind in the presence of her father.

Still, his assessment of her was pretty spot on, not that she'd ever admit that to him. The one thing that stuck in her craw was his insistence she was a romantic. Of course, he'd qualified it by saying she wouldn't think so, and that was also true. But as a child, one of her favorite pastimes had been having imaginary weddings to teen heart throbs in her back yard. Every Backstreet Boy had been immortalized in poster form on her walls, sending her off to sleep with dreams of kissing each and every one of them. When various boyfriends brought her flowers and tried wooing her, she always enjoyed it immensely, even if the boy in question was rather meh. No doubt about it, she loved being romanced. Too bad a certain sexy redneck didn't have a romantic bone in his body.

But did romance really matter? Sure, it was nice and fun, but love was love, regardless of all the frills. She didn't need mushy poetry, chocolates and flowers, or grand gestures. What Persia had always wanted was something she'd never received from her father—honesty. That mattered more than all the rest combined. And though it had taken him a while to reveal his true nature—

understandably—Warren had told her the truth about everything.

Her heart lurched in her chest, causing her to stumble, though she played it off like she'd tripped over a root. Her own truth was that she hadn't fully realized she wasn't just hot for the sexy carpenter. A part of her that had been buried so deeply she hadn't even known it existed surged with affection for him. When she recalled climbing aboard the van earlier, her breath hitched in her chest recalling the pain she'd felt leaving him in the dust like that. And not just because of the pain he most certainly felt after baring his soul to her, but because *she* hurt leaving him. They'd only been apart an hour or so and yet she longed to have him nearby. Not just for sex, but her soul ached for him.

Oh shit, I'm in love!

The thought startled her back into the present. Her father was still droning on about how much she meant to him, blah blah blah, as they neared the clearing where she'd met with Warren's wolf so many times.

"Enough, Daddy. Just stop already."

"Okay..." he conceded, though he clearly didn't want to.

She stopped just before they were about to break into the spot that felt so sacred to her. Sharing it with her father when he wanted to destroy it seemed wrong. Unless she could change his mind.

“Please leave Wolf Woods alone,” she pleaded, opening herself up to him so he could get a tiny inkling of how important it all was to her. “*Please.*”

“Now, princess—”

“Seriously, the chicken ranch is so much better for everyone. It’s a classic win-win-win, and you know it.”

Dick sniffed and wiped dirt off the toe of his very expensive loafer. “I can’t deny it’s a solid proposal, but I’m afraid it’s too little, too late, Persia. I’ve already poured way too much into this property.”

“In the form of bribes, perchance?”

He didn’t even have the grace to blush. He simply let his smirk answer the question.

“Do you want me to get down on my knees and beg, Daddy? Because I will.” She proved her point and dropped to the spongy forest floor, casting a pleading gaze up at him. “Please, if not for the locals, then for me. This isn’t just one of my causes, Daddy. It’s become so much more. It’s a mission of love.”

“Love?” he asked, his brow furrowing as if the concept was alien to him.

“I…” She cleared her throat and tried again. “I’ve grown close to one of the men from the, uh, Soren village. These woods mean so much to them, which makes this very personal to me.”

Dick's face grew red and then darkened to an apoplectic purple. "Y-you…" he stammered, unable to find words for whatever was bothering him. "You're in love with one of those filthy, fucking *mutants?*"

It took several moments for her father's words to sink in. When they did, Persia stumbled to her feet awkwardly and edged away from him. The horrific realization that her father knew what Warren and his people actually were rocked her to the core.

"You know?" she asked, her voice barely above a whisper.

Dick didn't bother denying it. Instead, he gave her a condescending glare, which spoke volumes. "Of course. What kind of businessman would I be if I didn't learn every single detail about my enemies?"

The full gravity of this information nearly made her heave. Swallowing hard, she asked a question even she, a die-hard Dick McNish hater, never thought she'd ask.

"So, you *knew* the wolves your hired guns have been hunting down aren't just animals?" Her hands flew to her mouth, wanting to take back the words as soon as they were spoken, but once they were out there, she recognized the truth in them. "Jesus, Daddy! You're killing *people!*"

"They're not people, Persia. They're mutants. Abominations that must be exterminated at all costs."

"No, they're not. They're just like you and me. They just have an unusual talent. They're good and noble and just want to live their lives without some fucking *murderer* shooting at them!"

Dick's face grew even more purple. "I can't believe you're defending *them.* I'm your damn father, Persia. Your blood!"

"Don't remind me," she spat back, finally and truly finished with the man who'd donated his genetic material once upon a time. "I'd rather spend the rest of my life as one of them than spend another minute in your toxic orbit!"

She turned to head back to her van, but Dick snatched at her arm, pulling her against him in a tight grip. His breath smelled of stale coffee and hate.

"My daughter will become one of those mutants over my dead body," he seethed.

Just as he started to drag her back the way they came, the bushes and small trees blocking her view of the meadow rustled frantically, and then a large, sandy-colored wolf bounded out of them. Dick shoved Persia toward the wolf in an effort to save himself, but Warren's wolf darted around her to position himself between her and her father. Paws splayed, head held low, lips pulled back in a terrifying, toothy snarl, he waited for Dick's next move.

The instinct to protect himself became secondary once he saw the wolf protecting Persia, his property. “Get away from my daughter, you *freak!*”

The wolf advanced a step, his hackles raised all the way along his spine. The low, rumbling growl coming from him grew into a sharp snap of his powerful jaws. Dick blinked in surprise, but when the wolf stayed put, he appeared to gain confidence, like maybe the beast had no plans to attack him at all.

“Time to finish this once and for all.” Dick sneered as he reached into his suit pocket and whipped out a tiny pistol.

Persia panicked. She’d spent her life wandering around, fighting her father for what she thought was right, but never putting down roots. She still had trouble wrapping her head around this shifter business, but Warren was worth the effort. So were the people in the Soren village… pack… whatever it was called. No way was she going to stand back and watch her father take that chance from her.

“No!” she screamed, grabbing fistfuls of Warren’s fur and trying to pull him behind her, but he was far too strong. He turned his massive head to look into her eyes, a sorrow that made her bones ache emanating from them, and then he bumped her with his hindquarters and sent her sprawling onto her ass.

"Dammit, stand still, you monster!" Dick shouted, trying to steady his sights on the wolf and not his daughter, though she remained dangerously close.

Just as he squeezed the trigger, a furry, black blur leapt out of the bushes, its huge body blocking Warren's wolf. A sharp yelp echoed through the canopy and a spray of blood splattered on Persia's face as the sound of the black beast crashing to the ground broke her heart. Whoever that wolf was, he'd just sacrificed himself to save Warren. That made him a hero in her book.

As Dick tried to make sense of the chaos, Warren took the chance to lunge forward and clamp down on the man's wrist. Dick tried to wrest free. Then he tried pulling the trigger again, but the pressure and pain proved to be too much. The gun thumped to the soft ground, his blood painting it crimson. Persia felt nothing but relief at her father's cries of pain as he stumbled away, toward the relative safety of his fancy car. Not that she wanted him to suffer… okay, maybe she wanted him to suffer a little.

Once Dick was far enough away to no longer be a threat, Warren shifted back into his human form. This time the transformation didn't freak Persia out as much as it had before. It was quite fascinating and sort of beautiful. Not to mention the fact he came out of his wolf form buck naked. But the moment his human eyes met hers, she realized other things were vastly more important at that moment. Such as the bleeding wolf lying in the dirt and leaves, the one who'd taken a bullet for her man.

"Levi." Warren's voice was tight.

They reached the wolf at the same time, Persia stroking his furry face as he whimpered in pain. "How bad is it?" she asked as Warren probed the wound in the wolf's shoulder.

He smiled reassuringly down at the wolf. "Levi, don't shift, okay? You need to conserve your strength. Doesn't look life-threatening to me, but we really need to get him to Trina."

Persia looked the massive wolf up and down. "How?"

"My truck's parked next to your van. I'll take his head. You take his tail." He crouched low to get a good grip on his friend.

Persia worked really, really hard not to laugh at the sight of a naked man nearly tea-bagging a buddy. It was just shock and hysteria working together to release some of the pent-up tension inside her, but even she knew how inappropriate the thought was. Warren watched her carefully, so to explain her obvious amusement, she pointed at the wolf's fluffy tail.

"Tails. Literally."

Ten minutes later, Persia's arms shook with strain as they gently laid the wolf on the ground between the vehicles. Her father's BMW was long gone, thank god.

"Are you sure he's going to be okay?" she panted heavily.

Warren checked the wound again, drawing a growl from Levi. "Yeah, bleeding's already stopped and you can see he's feeling pretty frisky."

"Then I really should go file that injunction. My dad's probably already scheming to crush us in some new way. Coward."

Worry flashed in Warren's eyes, and she quickly added, "But I'll head to Trina's right after. I swear. I'll be back."

He stepped closer, sweat dripping down his chest and weaving its way around his abs. "Are you sure?"

Locking her gaze on him, she reached for his hand. "Of course I'm sure."

Levi barked at them, reminding them he was lying there injured. They both jumped a little, embarrassed that they'd forgotten about him for a second.

"You should take my truck, it'll be faster. Besides, I think a naked man driving around with a bloody wolf in the bed of his truck might draw some attention. Keys are under the floor mat."

Persia nodded and quickly unlocked her van, grabbed her folder and tossed him the keys. Together they loaded Levi into her van, and then she gave his cheek a quick peck before heading to his truck, ready to show her father what she was really made of.

CHAPTER NINETEEN

Persia sang at the top of her lungs and totally off-key as she pulled Warren's truck onto pack lands near the end of the day. Strange not to think of it as an old homesteader's village because that was one hell of a cover, but stranger still, thinking in terms of a pack came naturally. It all seemed to fit so seamlessly.

All the more reason to celebrate the judge's order granting a temporary injunction against her dad. She'd broken every speed limit between the courthouse and pack lands so she could deliver the news. With demolition halted, it was only a matter of time before a different judge, one higher up the ladder, granted a permanent injunction. And it was all thanks to Warren and a particularly rare beetle.

Her dad would be livid when he found out, but she gave zero fucks about that. It was the least he deserved after all the misery he'd created. Right now, she and the pack needed something to celebrate.

As she parked in the gravel area outside the pack house, she spotted something that looked vaguely like Betty parked a little way behind the house, tucked up against the tree line. Climbing from the truck, she squinted, as if that might make her vision better.

"What the hell?"

As she drew closer, details came into focus and she couldn't believe what she was seeing. It was her Westfalia, all right, covered roof-to-tires in a vast array of flowers. Ceramic pots weighed down the roof. Vibrant blooms sprouted out triumphantly all over the bumper and tires. Bundles of loose wildflowers had been tied to every inch of space, and where they weren't, cornstalks leaned against any open spots. The tableau of flora made her home look like a rolling druid's shrine, and the twinkle lights wrapped around the roof several times gave the entire display an ethereal glow in the dusky twilight.

Unbelievable! *Someone*—as if she didn't know who—had gone to all this trouble and made this huge romantic gesture, just for her. Her throat tightened and she blinked away tears as she peered through a bare space on a window. No Warren, but the entire interior had also received the flowery treatment, with beautiful wildflower bouquets and rose petals scattered on the bed, which she noticed had been made up. A blush rose in her cheeks, not just from embarrassment, but also excitement over what the night would hold.

Music started playing behind her, an acoustic version of her very most favorite song in the world, *Endless Love.* Spinning around, she scanned the area, but she didn't see anything out of place—certainly no electronics that could be playing the music, not even an old-school boombox. Some shrubbery at the edge of the tree line rustled, and the moment Warren stepped out, Persia knew her heart belonged to him.

His rough hands strummed the simple chords on an old acoustic guitar slung over his shoulder as he closed the distance between. Then he opened his mouth and started singing.

"My love..."

Bold, clear, beautifully in tune. Tears sprang to her eyes and she didn't even care. She just wanted more. For a man who claimed to not be romantic, he certainly was proving himself wrong.

Persia had never in her life been serenaded. And as he strolled closer, she struggled to maintain her composure. Tears were one thing, but big, gut-wrenching, snot-flinging sobs might be the wrong message to send. When Warren shrugged in the most self-conscious way, she barked an incredulous laugh. He was nailing it, yet he still thought he sucked.

People filed out of the back door of the pack house to watch and listen. She barely noticed them. Her entire focus was on Warren. By the time he hit the second verse, he stood no more than a few feet away from her, so she joined in.

"Two hearts..."

Grinning like a blubbering madwoman, she stepped even closer and pretended her atonal voice sounded half as good as Warren's. She gave no shits. This was *their* song now. Every word spoke to how she felt about him, and she knew in her heart it did for him too. From that day on, she'd sing it as badly and as loudly as she could, every time she heard it.

By the time their duet ended, they both were singing loud and proud, claiming their endless love for one another. Cheers and whoops sounded from the pack house, followed by raucous applause—even the sound of a small dog barking—but Warren didn't so much glance in that direction.

Slinging the guitar behind his back, he closed the small gap between them and smiled down at her. She grinned right back, memorizing every inch of his face. In the distance, she heard a voice that sounded like Val's telling everyone to get back inside and give the love birds some privacy. Persia made a mental note to send the woman some flowers. Or maybe ammunition. Whichever she'd like best.

"Hey, Red," Warren murmured in his thick voice, his hand moving toward her as if he wanted to take her hand but then pulling back.

"Back atchya," she replied, closing the distance between their hands and entwining her fingers in his.

They stood inches apart, his scent wrapping around her like a cozy blanket on a chilly night. Uncertainty rolled off him in waves, echoed by the worry in eyes that resembled the sea on a clear day.

"I'm so sorry," he started, his voice low but firm. "I shouldn't have pushed you so hard. You need some time, and I get that. I'll chill out, I just hope you'll give me a chance to prove—"

Persia cut off his apology by pulling him into a fierce kiss. He froze for a moment and then wrapped his arms around her and pulled her tight. Their kiss turned deeper, his tongue slicking along her lips until she opened to him. The light in the sky darkened as they stood there kissing for the world to see, if the world was the slightest bit interested. That was fine by her. She wanted the world to know how much she cared for this brash, sexy, thoughtful, sweet country boy. And she hoped her kiss would show him too.

Finally breaking away, she took a few panted breaths before having enough air to speak. "I really don't need flowers and serenading to fall in love with you, Warren. You're pretty awesome, just as you are."

His slightly muddled expression turned deathly serious. "You might not need it, but by god, my mate's going to get it."

As if her heart hadn't been beating hard enough! Turning, she tugged his hand so he'd follow her. "Then we'd better get to that mating part. Don't you think?"

Apparently, that was all the encouragement Warren needed. He chuckled and scooped her into his arms, sweeping her off her feet in one fluid move. He carried her inside, kicking the door to shut it behind them. Even before it clicked closed, she had her arms wrapped around his neck, her lips on his once more. Their tongues tangled while he navigated the space, her arousal rising with each slide, dip, and taste of him. Soon they were in the bedroom, Warren lowering her feet to the ground before encouraging her to back up. She shuffled across the floor, unwilling to lose his touch for even a moment. He tasted too good, too perfect.

The backs of her knees hit the mattress and she groaned, happy they'd found a horizontal surface. Warren broke their kiss just long enough to slip the strap of the guitar over his head and then he was back, talented tongue tormenting her once more. She was sure he had set the guitar aside somewhere, but she couldn't care less. Not when his arms wrapped around her, hauling her close.

She reached for that torso that had taunted her this whole time and slid her fingers over the hard planes of his abs. She tugged and yanked on his shirt, exposing his bare skin to her palms. She explored his stomach, reveling in the feel of his heated flesh and deliciously carved muscles. She'd been denied long enough. She wanted to touch all of him, and she was going to, dammit!

Warren ran his fingers through her hair, and she sensed the loving desire in those large, rough hands of his. She lifted his shirt higher and pulled on the fabric, wanting it *gone,* and he understood, pausing long enough to rip it over his head and throw it aside. She swiped her tongue over his lips, taking in more of his taste. Sweet and hot and hers.

He gripped her waist and pushed her backward, tumbling onto the mattress, and she scrambled until she lay in the middle of the bed. He crawled after her, straddling her and cupping her cheek before capturing her lips for yet another kiss.

His thick cock pressed against her thigh, the hard length proving just how much he wanted her. The thought of his thickness had tormented her since they'd gotten so close to coming together. It'd only been three days and yet it seemed like a lifetime ago. It was a long, wild ride of passion and… love.

He reached for her breasts and she arched into his caress, anxious to have his mouth there—sucking, nipping, and tasting her. But just as he pinched a hard nub between his fingers, he released her and retreated. His brow furrowed, a hint of worry on his expression, and some of her need lessened. He gently grasped her chin in his hand, thumb stroking her lower lip.

"Are you sure this is what you want, Red?" His husky voice sent warm shivers down her spine.

"What's going to happen?" she breathed.

"I'm going to slide into you, fill this pussy." His voice made her want to get to that part right away, but she also wanted to know exactly what she was getting herself into. "And when we come—" *Yes, please.* "—I bite you."

"That's all?" she joked to hide a sudden bout of nerves.

"It's a mating bite. Once in a lifetime," he murmured. "It'll turn you into a werewolf and tie us together as mates." He lowered his forehead to hers, their gazes still locked. "There's no going back from this, Red. You have to be ready and I don't want to pressure you to take this step."

Persia tipped her head back and kissed him slowly this time, their lips melding in a sensual caress that conveyed her feelings better than words could. It was sweet and delicious at the same time and she stroked the side of his face as their passion was stoked once again.

She pulled away slowly, their stares meeting once more, and she released the words in her heart. "All I want is you."

The words hadn't been planned, but they were so natural, so right. They came from her heart and once they left her lips, she knew they were right. This felt right. And Warren's face practically glowed with her admission.

Warren descended on her as if the floodgates had burst open. He rained kisses down on her, tickling her and drawing a laugh. One that quickly turned into a gasp as he nipped her and released a low, rumbling growl. She should be afraid of the feral part of him—his wolf—but it only aroused her all the more.

He worked at her clothes, pulling and yanking until one after another, the pieces of fabric went flying through the air. Soon it was just the two of them—naked and bathed in the dim, romantic lighting.

Best of all was Warren's raw, masculine scent surrounding her, sinking into her lungs until no thoughts existed beyond him. She took a moment to look him up and down, kneeling over her, that thick shaft hard and ready to fill her. Then their gazes collided, and she found that his craving mirrored her own. Her heartbeat fluttered when he reached for her breasts, massaging and tormenting her with his passionate touches. He was possessive but this wasn't just about taking what was *his*. He caressed her and the more she allowed his hands to wander, the more loved she felt.

He kissed her breasts one at a time, capturing a nub between his lips and suckling the hard point. Each draw went straight to her pussy, her clit twitching and core clenching with the need to be filled. He repeated the caresses, drawing her need higher with each nip and suck until she writhed beneath him. She arched and pressed deeper into his mouth, wanting more from Warren. More and more and more…

He tilted his hips and rubbed his length against her pussy, his hardness stroking her while his hands and mouth remained occupied. Her slick pussy let him glide between her folds with ease and she shuddered as the tip of his length nudged her clit. His cock pulsed against her soaked flesh, drawing another tremble from her. He began slowly, savoring the touch as his tongue tormented her nipples again and again. His sharp teeth scraped one firm tip and she moaned deep, enjoying that bite of pain.

The thick crown of his cock flirted with her pussy, caressing her center with its mushroomed head. A promise of what was to come. Hopefully soon. She was ready for him. More than ready. She told him as much by grasping his hips and pulling him even closer. A silent message and plea in that one simple movement. One he obliged without hesitation.

A gasp of pleasure escaped her lips as he entered her, his hardness stretching her pussy, filling her in a single, punishing thrust. A snippet of pain came with the ecstasy and she moaned deep as he possessed her fully. He took control—took her. She was so slick with arousal that he slid into her to the hilt, not stopping the sensuous motion until their hips met. His thick girth filled her, touched her in places that she hadn't ever imagined. Her nerves were alight with the new sensations, the delirious ecstasy that came with his penetration.

"Don't hold back," she urged him, panting breaths coming between her words. "I want everything from you. I want it all."

Persia felt as if she played with fire and loved every moment. Loved it even more as Warren reacted to her words. He took one of her legs and turned her until she lay nearly sideways before him. He grasped her ass with a possessive hold while he fondled her breasts with the other hand—his touch dominant and loving at once. She had a moment to breathe, but only that moment, because then Warren turned his entire attention to driving her mad. He took control of her, her body, her pleasure.

"Oh god!" she rasped the words as he began truly punishing her, pumping his shaft in and out of her slick pussy.

He glided in and out of her, his hips snapping forward and pressing their bodies together in an intimate dance. His massive cock stroked her, deliciously raw yet caring as he fucked her hard, body jolting with every thrust. Nothing had ever felt more right. She clutched the sheets, needing something to ground her to the here and now as his attentions threated to destroy her with pleasure. Her mouth hung open, gasping for air, as he pounded into her.

The sound of his grunting pants and deep groans filled the air, the lewd slap of their bodies joining the sounds, and her face heated. His moans were all for her, every sweet, deliciously wicked sound was for her. This sweet, powerful country boy had it bad for her—as bad as she had it for him. A thought so fulfilling that tears threatened to push past the ecstasy assaulting her.

He thrust into her with exact precision, his cock grinding against her g-spot with relentless thrusts. He gave her more and more and more and she took every ounce of pleasure. She hoarded the sensations, gathering them close as Warren played her body like an instrument.

She'd demanded everything and it seemed he was ready to deliver.

Tension coiled inside her, gathering and building, coalescing into an ever-increasing ball of sensation. She gripped the sheets, struggling against the massive bubble that threatened to overwhelm her. It was so big. So much. So… Her pussy clenched around Warren's cock, milking his hard length and causing the gathered pleasure to increase in size with every ripple.

Soon. She was so close. She…

Warren rolled her to her back once more, his pace not faltering or changing in any way, but it was enough to send her release stumbling back. The impending ecstasy stuttered, and she struggled against him, fighting to reach the precipice once more. She'd been *so damned close...*

"Are you ready?" he growled—*growled*—and the truth of what came next hit her full force.

She was ready to come, but she didn't think that was what he meant. He wanted to make sure she was *ready*. Ready to be his. Ready to be a mate. Ready to be a werewolf.

The answer to it all was a single word, "Yes."

To make sure he understood, she tipped her head to the side, exposing more of her neck and shoulder. She wanted this—wanted to be his entirely.

His body continued to torment hers, his cock thrusting in and out of her pussy as he leaned down. He braced his weight on his hands and drew nearer, not stopping until their chests met and his lips hovered over Persia's neck. His breath fanned across her sweat dappled skin, a fleeting chill racing across her. She was possessed by him, surrounded by him, consumed by him.

Warren nuzzled her, his lips caressing the column of her throat, teeth nibbling her earlobe and then mouth ghosting over the shell of her ear as he whispered three words.

"I love you, Red."

Persia's response was automatic and instantaneous. "I love —*fuck!*"

Teeth pierced her flesh, sinking deep into her shoulder and sending searing pain through her body. Agony wracked her for a moment, stealing her breath and all other sensation, overwhelming her with the sudden injury. But it didn't stay painful for long. Her body knew better than her mind, the sensations transforming from agony to arousal and wanting.

The orgasm she'd been chasing surged once more, pushing and pulling her to the precipice. Pleasure renewed and leapt beyond the pain of the mating bite and drew her onward toward release. The bubble of joy swelled and grew once again, stretching until it felt near to bursting and she held her breath as she waited. Waited to be flung off the cliff into a sea of ecstasy.

Warren bit down harder and sucked on the mating bite, giving her more of that bone-melting bliss rather than the agony expected. The mating turned that soul-devouring hurt into the ultimate need and want and...

And a kaleidoscope of sensation enveloped her. The growing bubble of joy exploded and stretched to consume her. The pleasure extended to consume every inch of her, expanding to infuse her body from head to toe. She lost all sense of control, her muscles twitching and contracting without thought or intent. The inexplicable bliss snatched her free will and she became a slave to the ecstasy.

Her pussy milked Warren's cock, caressing and stroking his length with her inner walls. Each ripple extended her release, drawing the pleasure out even more. She panted and moaned as the bliss washed away every thought, leaving her a mindless mess of uncontrollable joy.

And amid the deliciousness, Warren found his own release. His hips twitched and pace stuttered, thrusts growing rougher for a moment as he chased his own orgasm and then he sealed their hips together. His thick cock pulsed inside her, a new heat bathing her slick channel, his cum coating her inner walls. He coated her in his scent, inside and out, and she'd never been happier or more at peace.

They'd made love. He'd bitten her—claimed her. Now…

He slowly withdrew his teeth from her flesh and lapped at her ragged flesh. One lick and then two before he whispered two words that she wanted to hear for eternity.

"You're mine."

CHAPTER TWENTY

THE DAY COULDN'T HAVE BEEN MORE FABULOUS. NOT ONLY was the sky blue, without a trace of rain clouds anywhere, the temperatures remained mild all day and the humidity was unusually low. Couldn't ask for much more for a party in rural Georgia.

More people than Persia could count milled about on the pack house lawn, chatting and laughing and generally having a great time. Pups, as she'd learned werewolf children were called, ran around like wild animals, even in their human form. A surprising number of adults semi-surrounded the pups, clearly wanting to keep them safe from the dangers her father had inflicted on them yet relaxed enough to let them still be kids.

The party's primary reason for being was to celebrate Levi's clean bill of health. He'd mostly recovered from his gunshot wound, thanks to Trina's ministrations and Dick

McNish's terrible aim. As Warren had suspected immediately, the wound was little more than superficial, but any gunshot wound could be deadly, it seemed, even to werewolves. And the bullets didn't even need to be made of silver!

Zeke had acknowledged Levi's sacrifice when he'd tried to protect Warren and Persia and had restored his status in the pack. He'd almost certainly never hold a position of power as he did when he was a member of the pack's Ruling Circle, but at least he was no longer assigned to poop patrol in Wolf Woods. Hopefully no one would be since Persia had managed to snare that temporary injunction. Plus, she had more up her sleeve that Zeke wanted to keep under wraps for the moment.

As she strolled through the crowd, meeting new people and greeting old friends alike, she felt more love than she ever had in her entire life. She'd felt unwanted and unloved most of the time, yet these people who barely knew her seemed to accept her without question since she and Warren had mated three nights before. No doubt about it, Persia finally felt like she'd found her place in the world. It almost made her sad, thinking about all the years she'd never known what happiness truly meant.

As she stood chatting with Hux Davenport, his wife—scratch that... *mate*—Marsha and their son Little Hux, Warren's head popped up above the sea of people. He waved and then disappeared. Soon he was by her side, slipping his hand into hers and listening intently as Little Hux prattled on endlessly about the puppy his daddy was going to get for him, and it was going to be just like Fang. Hearing her name, the little Pomeranian yipped from somewhere nearby, drawing chuckles from the little group.

"Oh wow," Warren looked over Persia's head across the crowd.

She turned and stood on her tiptoes, trying to see what had him so excited, but such was the life of a snack-sized gal. "What?"

"It's Chloe," he smiled down at her.

"Chloe? You mean that girl you used to have a big, fat crush on until you got a whiff of me?"

He pulled her into his arms and kissed the tip of her nose with a smile. "That's the one."

"I don't have anything to be jealous about. Do I? Because this whole new wolfy thing has me feeling things in a much bigger way. Just give me some warning if I need to release my she-wolf so she can kick some ass."

She was only half-joking.

Warren threw his head back and guffawed. "No, none at all. I had no idea what I was really feeling for Chloe. It certainly wasn't anything compared to how I feel about you. Like, at all. You're the only one for me, Persia."

A short redhead, escorted by a handsome tall man, made their way through the crowd until they found Warren. Persia gave in to a primal need to check out her competition, and one scan made her raise an eyebrow at her mate. She and this Chloe chick could have been sisters. Her mate certainly had a type. He simply smiled and slid the hand on her back low enough to caress her ass, which sent her into a tizzy of desire. Damn these unruly emotions of hers!

"Warren!" Chloe cried, smiling up at him but not hugging him, as Persia might have expected.

He tightened his grip on her ass, which only served to tighten her nipples in a most embarrassing way.

"Chloe, it's good to see you again. How are you, Drew?"

Chloe's mate stuck out his hand at Warren, which forced him to remove his from her butt. Oh well…

"Good to see you, man. What's new with you?"

A smile lit up Warren's face as he looked down at Persia. "I'd like you to meet my mate, Persia McNish."

"Persia *Edgecomb*," she corrected, thrilled to have a new name.

Chloe squealed in delight as Drew gave him a congratulatory slap on the back. Persia suddenly found herself in a tight hug with her supposed rival, draining any hint of jealousy out of her.

"I knew it," Chloe exclaimed in Persia's ear. Thankfully she pulled away and grinned up at Warren before shouting. "I fucking *knew* it! See, I told you you'd find your mate one day."

"Hey there, sailor," Val rushed up to her best friend since college and gave her a bear hug.

"You must forgive my sister, Persia," Zeke sidled up to Chloe and draped an arm over her shoulder. "She used to be a school teacher in Tremble and never uttered a single cuss word. Ever since Drew came along and lured her away from her family, she's developed quite the potty mouth."

Chloe elbowed her brother in the ribs, drawing a dramatic "Oomph!"

Fang growled at the "attack" on her alpha, earning amused chuckles from everyone except Little Hux. He hunkered down and played with the dog while the grown-ups chatted.

"Ignore my dumb, big brother, Persia. I'm just so happy Warren was patient enough to wait for you."

"Patience is everything." Drew pulled his mate into a side hug and gazed at her with the kind of devotion Persia had always envied. Until Warren had come along.

"Speaking of patience," Warren said, clearly trying to change the subject, "I hear you two are foster parents now?"

"Yes," Chloe glowed with happiness, "we're fostering twin boys whose parents were killed in a car accident."

Warren blinked in surprise, and Chloe held up a hand. "I know. Ironic, right? But it really feels like fate that they ended up with us."

"Chloe's such an incredible mother," Drew gushed.

"And you're a terrific dad," she replied. "We're on track to legally adopt them, but there's a lot of paperwork and hoops to jump though. It'll be worth it in the long run though."

"Chloe!" cried a voice through the mass of bodies.

Trina came bursting into their little group, a harried Max following closely behind. As everyone greeted one another, Warren pulled Persia in front of him, wrapping his arms around her waist and clasping them together. She settled her head against his chest and relaxed into his heartbeat.

"So, when are you two going to start making a bunch of adorable rogue pups of your own?" Chloe asked Trina and Max with a wink.

Trina quickly ducked her head and tucked a stray lock of blonde hair behind her ear. Max shot her a glance and then looked up at the sky, obviously avoiding everyone's gaze. Chloe gasped and clapped her hands merrily.

"Are you shitting me? This really *is* a day for celebrations. Isn't it?"

As they caught up, a line formed to greet the newest member of the pack—well, *almost* member. Persia found herself totally immersed in the warmth and connection they all seemed to share. The groups she'd become accustomed to over the years seemed to fracture or downright implode after a couple of weeks, but everyone in the Soren pack seemed to honestly care about each other's happiness and well-being. Naturally, not everyone could be best friends, but they were more like a family. They may get under your skin now and then, but you were still willing to give up your life to save theirs.

Even newbies related to their sworn enemy were treated like family. She lost count of how many pack members had thanked her for all the work she'd put in trying to save Wolf Woods. It was almost as if they sensed where her true loyalties lay, and considering her ridiculously heightened senses—some of which she still couldn't control or decipher—they probably did.

"So, what are your plans now that you're chained to old Warren?" asked one of Val's sentries with a teasing smirk.

She couldn't recall his name—Norman?—but he was easily identified by the faint pink circle smack in the middle of his forehead. With this group, the story of that circle was probably worth hearing and she made a mental note to ask Warren about it later.

"I'll have you know, Newman," Warren spoke, reminding her of the man's name and reminding Newman he was speaking to a mated female, "the NRC has already recruited my amazing mate as a legal consultant. She's going to ensure all pack lands around the country are properly defined and deeded, so no one can ever dispute their territories and force them from their lands again."

Newman looked impressed. "Wow, big job."

"It's not going to be easy," she acknowledged, "and might mean traveling to other packs on occasion, but I'll be damned if I watch anyone else try to do what my father's been doing. It'll probably take a few years, but it will be worth it in the long run."

Warren gazed down at her with pure adoration that set her heart fluttering. "Generations to come will have Persia to thank for protecting their lands."

Dusk had settled over the gathering and tiny twinkle lights decorated nearby trees, offering a touch of light and a festive atmosphere. Zeke stood on the porch and raised his hands. No need to shout or call everyone to attention because the simple gesture caught everyone's attention. Even Persia felt a weird tug in her chest to look his way. Probably some shifter thing. She had so much to learn!

“Listen up, party people! We are a very lucky pack. Our family is growing larger and stronger every day, and we have a number of people to thank for that. Namely, we have Persia McNish to thank. Don’t let her last name fool you. She has gone above and beyond to prove her loyalty to us. Using her passion and her legal expertise, she might just save Wolf Woods for good, and by extension, our pack lands, as well.”

The whole crowd cheered, and Warren hugged Persia close as happy tears stung her eyes. But Zeke wasn’t finished yet.

“But that’s not all she’s done for us,” he declared. “Persia is also moving forward with plans to have the state designate Wolf Woods as protected lands, so it will never be at risk again.”

More cheers erupted through the crowd with all eyes on Persia, who blushed furiously and tried her hardest to hold herself together. All the warmth and affection being directed at her felt like a warm cocoon but sensing others’ emotions about her was still so new, it threatened to overwhelm her.

“And just in case anyone was wondering, tonight Persia will officially become the Soren pack’s newest member when she accepts the loyalty vow.”

Zeke joined everyone in applauding as he waved her up to the porch. Shyness had never been one of Persia’s finer qualities—or faults, depending how one looked at it—and it was in short supply that evening. Mostly because she was so freaking overjoyed to have finally found a family who cared about her and respected her. No one had given her a choice about her birth parents, but she sure as hell could choose her family now, and not a single question remained in her mind that the Soren pack was where she belonged.

The ceremony was blissfully short, yet full of love and pure joy. Her vow would require her to put the welfare of the pack before all else, including her own life, to which she agreed readily. Two pack members had already risked their lives for her before she'd even become a wolf, and she knew the rest of them would too. It only seemed right for them to hear from her own lips that she would do the same.

At the end of the ceremony, while everyone cheered and howled their approval, Persia flew down the steps and into her mate's arms. They held on tightly, breathing each other in and savoring the moment as they tuned out the well-wishers. Finally, Warren pressed a kiss to the top of her head.

"I hope this doesn't sound condescending," he murmured into her hair, "but I'm so proud of you. So proud you're mine."

She pulled back so she could grin up to him, ignoring the tears streaming down her cheeks. "Me too… *my love.*"

He threw his head back and choked out a laugh thick with emotion. Then he brought his lips to hers and all she wanted was to be alone with him. Maybe no one would notice if they disappeared in the chaos. Just for a little while. An hour, two tops.

As she reached for Warren's hand to drag him through the crowd, her phone buzzed silently in her pocket. Nah, sex with her hot mate took precedence over a text. Then it buzzed again.

Odd.

"Sorry, one sec," she pulled her phone from the back pocket of her jeans.

The smile that had seemed permanently affixed to her face slid away as she read a series of emails from her connection at the courthouse. Anger replaced her joy and then fury took over. *Of course this would happen today, of all days,* she thought bitterly.

"Shit," she spat, tears of rage burning her eyes and her stomach threatening to unload all over the party.

"What's wrong?"

"The judge who was supposed to take several weeks to research our request for a permanent injunction against my dad just denied it out of hand."

Warren's face paled and his jaw literally dropped open. "Are you kidding me? What's that mean?"

Persia met his gaze, not even trying to sugarcoat the situation. "It means my father is free to start tearing down trees first thing tomorrow morning."

Warren scrubbed a hand over his jaw and through his hair as he glanced around the happy gathering. "I don't get it. I thought your case was iron clad. What happened?"

"You know, I thought the judge's name rang a bell when I heard the case had been assigned to him, but I didn't make the connection till now." Acid roiled low in her throat over her naïveté. "He's one of my dad's old golfing buddies."

CHAPTER TWENTY-ONE

AMBER LIQUID SWIRLED AT THE BOTTOM OF DICK MCNISH'S glass as he stared into the depths of his fourth Scotch of the night. Throwing back the last of it in one smooth motion, he rested the crystal glass on his polished mahogany desk and trained his hazy gaze across his large study to where the bottle sat. Maybe four was enough.

His first drink of the night had been to celebrate his victory over Persia's attempt to block progress. He'd even smiled as the smooth, smoky liquor slid down his throat and warmed his body from the inside out. The second drink had been to reinforce his belief he was actually celebrating. The third drink had turned his thoughts inward, never a good thing. And as the remnants of the fourth drink still tingled on his tongue, Dick couldn't help feeling as if he was subconsciously drowning his sorrows.

Ridiculous! He had nothing to be sad about. He'd won!

But at what cost?

He hated that little voice in his head. He'd spent most of his adult life ignoring it, to his great gain, and he had no intention of listening to it now. Not when he'd just managed to get everything he wanted.

Dick let his gaze slide around the room to remind himself of how far he'd come. The genuine Tiffany lamp sitting on his massive desk cast just enough light to create creeping shadows all around. He'd paid far too much for the damn thing at auction, just to piss off a competitor. Its delicate glasswork and feminine colors seemed out of place in his masculine, wood-paneled office, but he refused to sell it. It said something about him, something he'd longed for all of his life. It told anyone who laid eyes on it he was important.

Aside from the lamp, the room was exactly what he'd imagined for himself as a young man who'd put himself through business school. Heavy antique furniture lent a gravitas to the room, bolstered by a Persian rug worth a small fortune, a burgundy leather loveseat poised in front of a darkened fireplace, built-ins full of old books, and a mini-bar stocked with even older Scotch.

Even the house was old. Naturally, after closing on it, his wife Patricia had immediately called in an army of contractors and interior designers to update the place, but they couldn't erase all evidence of its age—as Patricia had managed to do with her face. Just like his aging bones, the house still creaked and groaned at odd moments. Patricia loved to gripe about it, but Dick had long ago learned how to tune out her and the creaks.

As he stood from his leather Eames chair, one such groan came from the depths of the house. A smile tickled the corner of his mouth, wishing Patricia wasn't lounging on some beach in St. Barts just so she'd be irritated that money hadn't solved that particular problem.

Empty highball glass in hand, Dick wandered over to the window overlooking his perfectly manicured and beautifully landscaped lawn. Another Patricia project, one he'd grown rather fond of over the years. The blackness outside only allowed him to see his own reflection, though, and that was something he couldn't stomach. Not tonight.

Turning away, a framed photograph perched on a bookshelf caught his eye. The Dick McNish in the photo looked far more familiar to him, though very little of the man he used to be still remained. A young and beautiful Patricia appeared annoyed as a small bundle of energy with a shock of vibrant red curls reached for someone just out of frame. Dick remembered that day, and he also remembered immediately firing the nanny Persia had been crying for.

He set down the frame and moved to the center of the room, bewildered over how his dream study had turned into a tomb that trapped him with his own demons. Only in the dim light of his private sanctuary could he admit he'd been a shitty father. Of course, he'd been a shitty husband too, but he and Patricia had known what they were getting into when they'd wed. It had been a business arrangement, but that had been their choice. Persia never had a choice. She'd been dealt a shitty hand, and a soul as sweet as hers deserved better.

Somehow, she'd wandered through the darkness of her childhood and into the light. She'd found a path that fulfilled her, and Dick couldn't help admiring her dedication. Her bull-dog tenacity came from him, that much he could claim, but where the hell did her rock-solid ethics come from? Certainly not from her morality challenged parents. Maybe Disney movies, or the many nannies who'd basically raised her.

Whatever the reason, he was proud of her. She rarely won against him, but he considered their little skirmishes to be a chess match. One day the student would become the master. She almost had, with that ridiculous beetle ploy. A pang of guilt wriggled deep in his gut, but he sniffed it away. He'd been holding onto a big, fat favor from an old friend for nearly two decades, just waiting for the right moment to call it in. He'd cornered her king and called checkmate.

Persia needed to toughen up and play dirty, at least a little. If she had, she might just have won. But she hadn't seen the playing board for the pieces. Just as with chess, Persia needed to learn the unspoken rules of the game before she could ever truly succeed. Those rules had been invented to separate the sheep from the wolves.

He snorted softly at the irony and looked forlornly into his empty glass. Fixing his relationship with his daughter might be a fantasy, but filling an empty glass was easy. Shuffling over to the bar, he *filled* the glass. Hey, it was a celebration, right?

The long sip of warm Scotch should have chased away the cold, which had settled on his heart. It should have made him feel better, more relaxed, but he was more tense than ever. Maybe once he got to the bottom of the glass again… or he'd simply pass out.

Either or.

If it was to be the latter, his Eames would be far more comfortable than collapsing to the hardwood floor. When he turned to retreat to the plush chair, he froze. Adrenaline spurted into his blood stream before his brain could even make sense of what his wide eyes were staring at.

Seven huge wolves stood around the room, their eyes gleaming with bloodlust and their fangs bared.

Uncontrollable tremors wracked his body and the full-to-the-brim glass slipped from his fingers at the same moment his bladder let loose. His sluggish brain was briefly grateful that the scent of the Scotch would overpower the smell of the urine spreading across the front of his bespoke slacks. Then he realized he would probably be dead in a matter of seconds, so it didn't matter.

He shot a glance over to his desk, where his gun lay in the top drawer, but a big, light brown wolf he recognized stood between him and the desk. The hackles running along the spine of the wolf stood on end, and his snarl turned into a guttural growl. It looked as if the son of the mutant he'd killed months ago would finally get his revenge.

And all he could do was stand there and piss himself.

Another wolf, this one shorter and stockier than the others, and with ginger-colored fur, stepped toward Dick, sending him into a full-blown panic. His knees buckled out from under him, sending him sprawling to the floor.

"P-please!" he screamed, waving his hands over his head in surrender.

Scrambling backward, he curled himself into a tight ball in the corner before daring to peek up at the ginger wolf. It had something in its mouth, but his fear and the darkness made it impossible to identify. Besides, unless it was some kind of firearm, nothing could help him now.

"Please, don't kill me," he babbled, tears and snot and spit spraying everywhere. "I'll do anything! Just don't kill me!"

Deep down, he was surprised by how quickly he'd conceded, but money and power meant nothing when you were staring Death in the face. Or in his case, seven versions of Death.

When the ginger wolf took another menacing step forward, he ducked his head between his arms and started sobbing. Any second now, sharp teeth would pierce his flesh and tear him apart. Probably slowly. And for the first time in his life, he admitted to himself he deserved it.

Hot breath feathered against the bare skin of his arms, but instead of pain, he felt something light fall onto his balled-up body and slide to the floor. He waited. And waited. Nothing more happened, not even any sounds. Daring to take a peek, he found the ginger wolf looming over him, its face in shadow, but there was enough light to see its lip pulled back far enough that drool dripped out and onto…

Was that a file folder?

Clearly the beast wanted him to look at it, so he very slowly reached for it and opened it. For a few seconds, his eyes couldn't focus on the document inside because they continually flicked back up to make sure the wolves weren't advancing on him. Then a specific word caught his attention, then another. Soon the words turned into sentences and paragraphs that made sense, yet...didn't.

He scanned the pages as he flipped through them and then glanced up at the ginger wolf before going back to the beginning and reading the legal document more thoroughly. The attorney of record was listed as Persia Edgecomb. By the time he finished, the ginger wolf had taken two steps back. The light reflecting off the bar's mirror shone on the animal's face, and with a start, Dick realized it had one brown eye and one blue. Just like...

"Princess? Is that you?"

Another huge wolf—not the biggest in the room, but still bigger than the average dog—advanced and stood shoulder-to-shoulder with the ginger wolf. Dick recognized it as the same one who'd jumped in to protect Persia, the same one he'd tried to shoot. It had to be the freak she'd talked about loving. Anger overpowered Dick's fear.

"You motherf—"

Before he could finish, or so much as move, the wolf version of Persia lunged forward. *Snap!* Dick recoiled in terror as her jaws snapped so close to his face he felt her whiskers. Cringing back, he tried to focus on her.

"What do you want from me?"

The wolf near the desk, the one who obviously wanted to kill him, stood on his hind legs and grabbed Dick's fountain pen between his teeth. Slowly, as if to torture him, the animal stalked toward him and then dropped the pen in Dick's wet lap. He picked it up and looked at it as if he'd never seen a pen before. Then he looked at the folder. Then at Persia-wolf.

"You've got to be fucking kidding me, Persia. You want me to sign a purchase agreement for that goddamn chicken ranch?"

Maybe it was the realization that his soft-hearted daughter was leading this little foray, or maybe it was the influence of the first gulp of his fifth Scotch, but Dick finally found his balls.

"No fucking way," he started, sitting up a little straighter and covering the mess in his pants with the folder. "I already told you, I'm not—"

The other five wolves advanced as one, joining Persia-wolf and her...whatever he was called. They snarled in unison, sending fear as hot as molten silver into Dick's veins. Then they took a step toward him as one symbiotic unit.

"Stop!" he screeched, not recognizing his own high-pitched voice.

They all paused mid-step, each wolf's right paw held inches over the floor, as if they'd practiced the move. Dick froze too, unsure if he was pissed or proud. Both? Didn't matter. He was a dead man if he didn't agree to move his development to the abandoned chicken ranch on the other side of Tremble, that much was clear by the hate burning in six sets of lupine eyes. The seventh…well, she'd always had a loving heart he'd both cursed and admired.

Unscrewing the cap on his Montblanc fountain pen, Dick scribbled his name or initials on all the pages Persia had marked with stickies and then tossed the folder at her feet. Er… *paws.*

"There! Happy now?"

Persia-wolf's bi-colored eyes narrowed to slits as she closed the gap between them. Dick ducked and covered his head, waiting for his inevitable death. He prayed to a god he'd never believed in for it to be quick. He'd already experienced a taste of what a wolf could do when the one next to Persia had bit him in the woods, so he knew it wouldn't be painless. After all he'd done, he had little doubt she would rip out his jugular and let the rest feast on his carcass.

Clamping his eyes shut, Dick waited for his just desserts. Whatever dignity he'd had in the seconds before the wolves surrounded him had soaked the front of his pants. He was ready for the end.

But instead of tearing flesh and spurting blood, one very big, very warm, very wet tongue traveled the length of his face, from the base of his jaw, all the way up his stubbly cheek, to the top of his head. Slimy wetness dripped down his face as he opened one eye to find Persia-wolf panting happily in front of him.

Gingerly picking up the file folder with her teeth, she wagged a fluffy, ginger tail as her gaze softened. One by one, five of the wolves sauntered out of Dick's study, leaving only Persia-wolf and the sandy one whose name she'd taken. He stood in the doorway, keen eyes watching Dick as Persia-wolf stood before him, her intelligent gaze searching his face. Sadness flickered there when she couldn't find what she wanted. Then she turned to follow the rest.

Dick watched her, still in shock that his own daughter had become one of *them*. They were freaks, aberrations, monsters! Yet, the way she'd talked about the guy she'd fallen for… He'd never felt such affection for anyone in his entire life, with the possible exception of Persia. He envied it. He envied *her*.

Maybe it wasn't too late. Maybe there was hope for them. Maybe there was hope for *him*.

"Wait," he whispered so quietly he barely heard himself, but Persia-wolf's ears twitched and she stopped.

Looking over her furry shoulder, she watched and waited.

Swallowing the lump stuck in his throat, Dick mustered his courage. "I'm glad you're happy, princess. I…" If ever there was a time to let his emotions show, this was it. Not bothering to choke back his tears, he continued. "I really do love you."

Persia-wolf whined softly and then followed her pack into the night.

If you enjoyed this book, please be totally awesomesauce and leave a review so others may discover it as well. Long review or short, your opinion will help other readers make future purchasing decisions. So, go forth and rate our level-o-awesome!

Want more from the bodacious duo of Celia & Marina? Check out *Having Her Enemy's Secret Shifter Baby...*

http://bklink.to/secretshifterbaby-buy

"Shots, Jane. *Shots!*" Elizabeth slurred and wrapped her thin arm around Jane's shoulders.

Jane Coleman smiled at her friend and unwound herself from Elizabeth's grasp. Elizabeth's breath could knock a fire-breathing dragon out of the night sky. "Don't you think you've had plenty? Come on. I want to dance."

"It's not me I'm worried about," Elizabeth complained, slouching to one side as she spoke, almost like a marionette without a puppeteer. "You've barely had anything to drink all night."

That, strictly speaking, was true. She'd had two beers on the beach earlier in the day and one Cosmo since they'd arrived at the bar, but she knew better than to get tipsy around her human friends. Tipsy werewolves were dangerous werewolves. Lowered inhibitions tempted her to shift into her wolf form. And as much as she loved the idea of sprinting down the beach, the sea breeze fluttering through her strawberry-blonde fur… the sight of a wolf running around a Ft. Lauderdale beach at the height of spring break might cause a panic. A tiny one.

Plus, after one too many, it was too easy to forget she had to treat humans like porcelain or she might accidentally hurt someone. Normal human girls—like she was pretending to be—weren't able to pick up a coffee table and chuck it across the room with one hand. Hell, her freshman year, she nearly tore a frat boy's arm clean off when he grabbed her ass at a party. She'd experienced a twinge of regret that he'd lost his baseball scholarship because she dislocated his shoulder, but he certainly learned never to grope a woman without her permission.

"You know I don't drink much," Jane reminded her friend. "I just want to dance." She tugged on Elizabeth's arm. "Come dance with me!"

Elizabeth slouched away like a ragdoll and bumped gracelessly against the bar. "Please? One shot. We'll toast to graduation."

"That's months away."

"Oh, please! Everyone knows you're going to graduate top of the class." Elizabeth rolled her eyes. "We should celebrate!"

Though Elizabeth's "celebrate" sounded more like *celibate* and Jane's wolf pawed at her. It was not a big fan of the word "celibate" and liked to remind her of that. Often.

"You're right, it's *you* we have to worry about," Jane teased. "Fine, one shot, but no more after this. One and *done*."

"Fine." Elizabeth sounded like her tongue was a little too big for her mouth. "What're we drinking?"

Jane smiled broadly at the bartender, which was all it took to grab his attention. He practically stopped mid-pour and rushed to them.

"What can I get you, ladies?"

"Two shots of Don Julio with lime and salt, please." Jane beamed and he blinked.

"Sure thing."

He dashed back to the other side of the bar, and Elizabeth snorted and rolled her eyes.

"What?" Jane frowned at her friend.

"You."

"What'd *I* do?"

"I think it's magic. You have some weird voodoo, dick whisperer, pied piper of the penis thing. It's like a supernatural power. You just have to think you want a guy's attention and then—" Elizabeth snapped her fingers. Or tried. She couldn't get her fingertips to touch each other and stared at her hand cross-eyed for a while before finally giving up and flailing her hands instead. "*Poof!* He's there."

Jane snorted as if Elizabeth's words were ridiculous. She couldn't let on that her friend was way too close to the truth. "I'm just like everyone else."

"Nope, uh uh, no way," Elizabeth said, as the bartender set their drinks in front of them.

"Thanks," Jane said with a flirty smile, tossing her long, strawberry blonde hair over her shoulder.

"No problem. This round's on me." He winked at Jane and then moved down the bar to help some other hapless maiden. It wasn't until he was out of sight that she noticed he'd written his number on her cocktail napkin.

"Smooth," Elizabeth sniffed. "How do I get them to do that? Or is it all about the boobage?" Elizabeth stared down at her own cleavage and jiggled her tits. "Do your job, dammit."

Jane laughed. "What are you talking about? You've got *great* boobs."

Elizabeth sighed, tossed back her shot, and then slammed the empty glass on the bar. She hissed as the tequila burned its way down her throat. "Don't pretend you're not built like one of those sexy mud flap girls."

Jane quirked a brow and slid the shot glass out of her friend's reach. "I think you've had plenty to drink now."

Elizabeth always got like this when she drank. As a lifelong dancer, her frame was lean and wispy. She had very little in the chesticle region and next to no junk in her trunk.

And her point of comparison?

Jane. Always Jane. Or mud flaps, but that always circled back to Jane anyway.

It was one of the human quirks Jane had never understood and her wolf woofed its agreement. In the pack, no one focused on appearance. Okay, maybe it was only Jane who didn't care. She'd never dressed to flaunt her bountiful curves. As the daughter of the alpha, it wouldn't be seemly—or so he insisted.

"Elizabeth, let's dance. I'm sick of standing around."

Elizabeth shook her head and wobbled precariously. "No way. I'm heading back up to the room. If I try to dance, I'll fall over."

Jane felt a whisper of disappointment at calling it a night so early, but her bestie needed her. "Okay, let's go."

Elizabeth shook her head. "No, you stay and have fun. Enjoy yourself. I'll see you in the morning."

Jane tracked Elizabeth as she made her way into the hotel and kept an eye on her through the floor-to-ceiling windows until she boarded an elevator. Then she turned her attention to the darkened beach. The bar sat on the edge of the sand, lights casting a soft glow across the beach.

A handful of lovebirds danced at the edge of the circle of light, kicking up the sugary powder as they moved and dancing slowly despite the rapid beat of the music. She was tempted to move to the black space just beyond them, where she could see the stars glittering on the ocean's surface like fireflies. Where she could be swallowed in the dark and enjoy being a faceless presence. She could do whatever she wanted and there wouldn't be anyone to tell her it was "unseemly."

Jane shook her head and made her way to the middle of the dance floor. She'd agreed to hit the bar with Elizabeth because she'd been promised dancing. Dammit, she was going to dance.

Shafts of light flashed in the delighted faces of the people crammed on the dance floor. The DJ's light show was synced with the music, flashing a different color with every beat while the crowd jumped and danced to the up-tempo song. Just as quickly as the energy rose, it gradually settled into a gentle sway when a slower song filled the air. Jane closed her eyes and lost herself in the music, feeling the notes flow through her while she found her rhythm.

This was her time, her chance to unwind before the end of her career as a college student. After that? Her life would begin. Her *human* life. She'd find a job in her field of study —*art history 4 lyfe*—and do her best to "fit in." Shifting wouldn't be a part of her life anymore. Her wolf whined like it always did and Jane fought against giving in to that pitiful cry. It knew she'd become immune to its pouting and switched to growls instead, snarling its objection. It didn't want to be turned into a second-class citizen inside her two-legged body.

She'd been born a werewolf. Why couldn't she just be happy being a werewolf?

Jane mentally sighed. She had plans. Eventually she'd find a nice human man with his nice, boring human life, and then they'd settle down with a house and a white picket fence.

Couldn't it see the benefit to a life in the suburbs? No fighting. No dominance games. No alpha telling her how to live her life or declare her actions "unseemly"?

She seriously hated that word.

Jane got back to reminding her wolf of "the plan."

Children were out of the question, of course. She'd heard that mixed-breed babies had more trouble controlling their shifts than full-blooded wolves. She wouldn't be able to hide her true nature if she had to control a feral child and she was determined not to risk being discovered.

Of course, her parents wouldn't like her decision, especially her domineering father.

Her wolf nudged her, telling her that it agreed with her dad and she shouldn't turn her back on her wolf heritage. She pushed the beast to the back of her mind, shoving it away from her surface thoughts. It retreated with an echoing growl, telling her that she should be thankful to have such a good alpha.

And her father really was a good alpha to the Coleman pack, but she couldn't wait to be out from under his thumb and away from Wilde Mountain. He expected so much from her… Too much. She'd never asked to be the daughter of an alpha, so why should she have to abide by his arbitrary rules?

Rejecting life in the pack would be unthinkable, as far as he was concerned, and she had no doubt he'd put up a fight.

A wave of sadness washed over her and she closed her eyes. Lights flashed orange behind her closed eyelids and she struggled to move with the blood-thumping beat of the music.

As much as she hated the idea of staying with the pack, she'd also miss her parents—her mother's smiling face and father's grumbles and growls. But she had no choice. She *would* live life on her own terms, and if her father couldn't accept that, she'd go somewhere her pack could never find her.

A hacker at school had already agreed to create her new identity… for a price. All that was left was to pick a place her family would never think to look for her and her life could begin.

And she only had a few months left.

Excitement overrode the twinge of sadness. Biting back a smile, Jane lost herself in the music again, rolling her hips along with the bassline and dropping low every now and then. Without anyone around her she felt freer than she had in years. She let her hair swish across her back as she moved.

But like all good things, it had to come to an end.

Something—*someone*—bumped against her back, and weak human hands slid around her waist. The stink of sweat, cloying cologne, and alcohol stung her nose and she tried to shimmy away, hoping the guy would get the hint and let her go.

He didn't.

Instead, he gripped her tighter, pulled her ass into his crotch and whispered in her ear. "I like the way you move, baby."

Baby? She wasn't his baby.

Her inner wolf wanted to turn around and teach the human male why it was a bad idea to lay his hands on a werewolf. With one hand, she'd grip his wrist so hard his bones splintered. With the other… she'd ensure baby-making wasn't in his future. Ever.

This stranger wasn't an alpha, hence, not worthy of her. Except… Accepting the touch of human males was part of assimilating into human life, right? No human male could compare to the strength of even the weakest wolf, much less the alpha her position in the pack demanded.

She groaned and her wolf snarled. She'd have to get used to being around weak men. It was a sacrifice she was willing to make if it meant living life on her own terms.

But that didn't mean they were allowed to rub their unimpressive members against her ass. Shaking her head, Jane gently pulled away. She wasn't going to make a scene by breaking the dude's arm. Unfortunately, the guy was an idiot. A drunk idiot, but still an idiot. He caught her wrist and tugged her back against him once more.

"Don't leave, angel. You're perfect right where you are."

“Not so much,” she yelled above the music.

“We’re just getting started.”

“No, you’re not.”

The voice was deep and gruff and unfamiliar, and it set the hairs on her arms standing on end. So much more masculine than the whining tenor of the man who’d been grinding up on her. The warm evening air whispered over the crowd, delicate flavors of the sea intermingled with the aroma of those around her. Then she caught his scent.

Not bland or vague like human men. He was all musk, mountain air, and leather. Scents that crept into her and taunted her wolf. Exactly the way a man ought to smell.

Jane craned her neck to get a good look at him, but only a dark shadow slanted out from a commandingly tall frame. In the span of a blink, the human was ripped away and this new man took his place. Strong hands grasped her hips and a muscular body aligned with her curves. She melted into his firm touch, moving with the music without thinking as she breathed him in. His scent teased and taunted her, making her head spin with the flavors.

God, nobody had smelled this tempting in years. Not since she’d left her pack. Not since…

She breathed deeper and caught a rustic woodiness that was all too familiar. If she didn’t know any better, she’d guess he was a wolf too. But that was impossible, right?

Of all the random bars in all the random states, what were the odds two wolves would wind up dancing together in the same beachside bar?

Jane's brain wanted her to turn and ask him, but her body wanted to continue moving in perfect time with his. So, she remained silent and let her body take the lead, reveling in the hard lines of his abs and a particularly tempting hardness against her ass. The more they danced, the more Jane was sure the man overwhelming her with his mere scent wasn't human.

He gripped her hips tighter as a new song began, and her wolf purred with happiness. With him snug against her, Jane ached for him to explore her body, to turn her around and let her feel every massive inch of his body hidden beneath his tight jeans.

Yet his hands stayed in place as her heartbeat soared.

Seriously? This was insane. She didn't even know what the dude looked like, but already her body howled for him to take her. She wanted him to run his work-calloused palms over her breasts and tease her right there on the dance floor. She felt more alive than ever—swaying with the music and allowing her body to move as she desired.

She rolled her hips, rubbing her ass against this man's growing need. Heat raced through her, a desperate throb taking up residence at the juncture of her thighs. She repeated the tempting move and figured it'd only be minutes before he finally lost control and took her. All she had to do was get him there.

The song switched again and a deep, rumbling bassline echoed the low pulse of need between her thighs. Swiveling her hips in time with the music, Jane pushed her ass up against him a hint harder, delighting in his surprised gasp.

"You're trying to tease me," he growled in her ear. That deep rumble had the tips of her breasts tightening into hard pebbles.

"Is it working?" she whispered in return.

Gripping her harder, he spun her to face him and held her just as snugly as he had before. She faced a broad wall of muscle covered by a loose linen shirt tucked neatly into a pair of snug jeans. It took every ounce of strength for Jane not to sink her fangs into his flesh and claim him. Hopefully he wouldn't see how badly she drooled at the idea.

It felt like it took a year for her to crane her neck far enough to meet the stranger's gaze. Then her heartbeat stuttered.

For a moment, all she could see were harsh lines, and then his feral beauty came into focus. His jaw was made of stone, and his light brown eyes held mesmerizing flecks of gold. She couldn't tear her gaze away, even if she wanted to.

Without a word, his eyes flickered from brown to a glowing amber, confirming her suspicions. Whatever the odds, he was a werewolf, and somehow they'd found each other. When she flashed her own amber eyes, he growled in approval.

"Thought so," he muttered, his eyes never wavering from hers—more amber than brown now. "Name?"

"Jane. You?"

"Reese."

The rumble of his animalistic voice sent another thrill of pleasure straight to her core. She could probably come right there if he'd just keep talking.

His next words took her right to the edge. "Let's go."

It wasn't a question and she didn't mind his demanding tone one bit.

Thick, warm fingers wrapped around her hand and Jane followed along eagerly as he led her through the crowd. His restraint at not tearing everyone in their way to shreds was admirable and everything, but Jane's wolf howled at her to get down to business already. She had a scratch that only Reese could reach. She wanted him more than anything or anyone else in her entire life.

Being so close to him, covered in his scent and body prepared to accept every inch of his cock...

Nothing had ever felt more right.

http://bklink.to/secretshifterbaby-buy

ABOUT THE AUTHORS

CELIA KYLE

Ex-dance teacher, former accountant and erstwhile collectible doll salesperson, New York Times and USA Today bestselling author Celia Kyle now writes paranormal romances. It goes without saying that there's always a happily-ever-after for her characters, even if there are a few road bumps along the way. Today she lives in central Florida and writes full-time with the support of her loving husband and two finicky cats.

Website

Facebook

~

MARINA MADDIX

New York Times & USA Today Bestselling Author Marina Maddix is a romantic at heart, but hates closing the bedroom door on her readers. Her stories are sweet, with just enough spice to make your mother blush. She lives with her husband and cat near the Pacific Ocean, and loves to hear from her fans.

Website

Facebook

Cover design by Clarissa Yeo of JoY Author Design Services.